PREDATORS ARE MY PREY

STARRING:
Sidney Jacobson & Clara Jacobson

GUEST APPEARANCE:
Lillian from The Splintered Doll

BY NICKI GRACE

The Twisted Damsel

ISBN: 9798452671572

To my Mom and Dad. Thank you for always helping me think outside the box, push past my limits, and never let circumstances determine the outcome. We are an odd bunch, and I wouldn't have it any other way.

CHAPTER ONE

"RAZOR BLADES CUT DEEP."

I made my way through the party. The asshole I was looking for had to be here somewhere. His name was Alexander Wright, and he loved the ladies.

In his defense, he was a 20-year-old college student, which meant partying, girls, and poor choices were his life.

Word around campus was that he had raped several girls, yet none had reported it. I think it's because they feared him and what he, or rather his family, could do. But I had no such fear.

Alexander was popular, rich, and, if I'm being honest, attractive.

Three things that would make it hard for an entire courtroom to believe he was a wolf in sheep's clothing, but not me. I believed the rumors. Not only did he look the type, but the stories were all the same. He gets the unsuspecting victim drunk, high, or whatever people are doing these days and takes advantage of them.

While my heart did go out to all of the girls he has wronged, it wasn't my place to correct him. Sadly, I had to mind my own business, which could be trying for me, but I managed it pretty well . . . until I didn't.

Either way, Alexander would have been safe from my

wrath. But he fucked up. Not figuratively, but literally. A few months ago, he raped my twin sister Clara. Unacceptable.

Clara was one of the sweetest people you could ever meet. She's quiet, shy, book smart, soft-spoken, and extremely kind—nothing like me.

For instance, I loved dressing sexy and experimenting with hair, makeup, etc. I was a bartender, so looking good was part of the job. I didn't mind a crowd, I loved being out in the world and having a good time.

Clara wouldn't be caught dead at a party, and if it weren't for her lab partner, Tori, she wouldn't have been.

They were late turning in an assignment, and Tori was supposed to have sent her portion to Clara, but she forgot and went to a fraternity party taking place that night. When Clara contacted her, she was apologetic about her screw-up, and fortunately, the hard drive was in Tori's purse, but unfortunately, Clara would have to come and get it.

So Clara went to the party and spent thirty minutes searching but never located Tori. Instead, she ended up meeting Alexander, who was "oh so concerned" that my sister was there alone and couldn't find her friend. Being the good guy that he was, he offered her a drink and said he would help her look.

Clara wasn't thirsty, but she thought it would be rude to decline. I had repeatedly told her that most people couldn't be trusted. But like I said, she's too nice.

A few minutes into looking for Tori, Clara started to feel dizzy, and Alexander offered her a quiet room to sit down in while he called her a cab. He did call the cab, but it was after he raped her.

She spent days crying and reliving not only this new incident, but also the abuse from our childhood. I tried to get her to report it, but she refused, not wanting the attention and problems it could bring. Eventually, I left her alone about it, deciding that if she didn't want vengeance to be hers . . . it could be mine.

"GET A TRASH CAN!" a girl yelled from somewhere to the right of me. Her hand was on the back of a shirtless guy hunched over, covering his mouth.

I stopped walking as another guy rushed in my direction, carrying the requested trash can. He almost made it too, but at the last second, Mr. shirtless vomited, and it splattered all over the floor and the lower half of an oversized dark-colored couch. It was slimy, chunky, and wet. Gross.

Someone next to me grabbed my arm. I glanced up into the face of a man way too old to belong at a party like this. He probably wandered in, looking for someone to score with for the night. He was barking up the wrong tree.

"Hey, baby. How's your night going?" he asked.

I counted to five, took a deep breath, and let it go. I know I dressed the part, sporting a low-cut half top and a short fitted skirt, but I was on a mission. Not to mention, I hated pet names from strange men, especially when they're only using it to get some ass.

It's sleazy, offensive, and makes me want to toss them into a giant meat grinder. I mean, did this guy honestly believe that referring to me by cutesy names would undo how filthy and untrustworthy he was?

"My night is fine," I responded, scanning the room in order to continue my search for Alexander. I tried to pull away, but he didn't let go.

"Whoa whoa, where ya going? I want to get to know you. Maybe we can find somewhere to talk."

He was holding my arm hostage. It wasn't too tight, but, still, who the fuck did he think he was?

I looked down at my arm and then back up at him. He

was maybe five-ten to six feet and slim, with a long beard. I was 5' 5" and 125 pounds. I could probably take him, but I wasn't dressed for the challenge, and it was too crowded in here.

So instead of kneeing him between the legs so hard it caused damage, I smiled and asked, "What's your name?"

He released his grip, apparently thankful that I had gotten with the program.

"J.D."

"Well, J.D.," I touched his chest lightly with my fingertips. "I'm at this party because last weekend I fucked this gorgeous guy that ended up giving me chlamydia," I tapped my chin, "or was it gonorrhea? Anyway, tonight I'm here to give it to someone else."

J.D. stared at me, highly disgusted as I continued on.

"I was hoping to find another football player, but I wouldn't mind letting you in on the fun. It does burn like hot acid when you pee, though, but I think you can handle it. Come on, let's go."

He swatted my hand from his chest.

"Fuck that!" he said and walked off.

I rolled my eyes. He was such a dumb ass.

I proceed to push my way through the crowd again. If I weren't so focused on finding Alexander, I'd be dancing with everyone else. My last good party was one that I attended with my coworker Cassie. Those were always an adventure.

I earned myself a few glances of appreciation from several guys I passed. I was used to the admiration and I loved how unthreatening it made me seem.

Damn, this place was packed. College students were everywhere, losing their minds and partying like there was no tomorrow. There was even a couple over in one corner having sex!

Now, I liked a good time, but sex wasn't my thing. I never understood the obsession with the act or even how people could do it so openly. Then again, I was a 20-year-old virgin and not interested in changing my status anytime soon, so what did I know?

Up ahead, I heard a shout that was momentarily louder than the blaring music. It was a guy standing on top of a table screaming obscenities before he jumped down into a group of people gathered near a barrel of beer. No one could say he wasn't having a good time.

I scanned the group of people around him and then . . . bingo. Alexander was standing across from the loudmouth, enjoying himself as if the incident with my sister, and God knows how many other women, had never happened.

I took a step forward, but stopped. The tape I had wrapped around my upper thighs was starting to cut off circulation. I knew adding that extra layer would come back to haunt me, but I had to protect my legs. I rubbed my outer thighs a few times through my skirt and kept walking.

There was a cup sitting on the edge of the counter in front of me, and I picked it up. The powerful scent of alcohol enveloped my sense of smell immediately.

"Hey!" Some girl in a yellow bikini top and light blue shorts said. "That's mine."

I stared at her. I did not have time for this bullshit. Alexander might get away, and I was starting to feel cramps from my period. This was not my night. Without breaking eye contact, I spit into the cup.

"Want it back?" I asked, offering it to her.

"Umm, no . . . you can keep it." the girl backed away.

I moved on in the direction of Alexander. As I approached the crowd, I loosened my hips to emphasize a side-to-side wobble, showcasing my instability to hold my liquor. Alexander was still cheering on the guy who had practically inhaled two cups of beer.

"Fuck yeah, Don! That's what I'm talking about."

Everyone in this area was shoulder-to-shoulder. I had to squeeze in really close to him to facilitate my accidental run-in. I hoped like hell the sexy heels I was wearing didn't get too messed up during this whole ordeal.

I had a slight shoe obsession, and it's the one downside to my revenge hobby. I bumped my arm into his and fell slightly forward onto him, then tipped the cup I was holding. Most of it got on his shirt and shoes. He jumped back and began wiping at his clothes.

"Oh, I'm so sorry!" I exclaimed. "I didn't mean to."

"Maybe if you were looking where the fuck you are going—" he began, but stopped as he looked up at me.

His whole demeanor changed, and he took a break from wiping his shirt. His eyes scanned me up and down, and I smiled nervously, displaying an expression of deep concern and worry.

He cleared his throat and shifted to the left, guiding me with him. The repositioning placed us outside of the tight party circle.

"It's no big deal, mistakes happen."

"I'm such a klutz. I swear I can't get anything right. Let me see how bad I got you."

I touched his shirt and winced at how soaked it was.

"Do you need me to have this dry-cleaned? I will completely understand if you do."

If this asshole says he wants me to have this shirt cleaned, I'm going to make my little surprise hurt even worse, I think to myself.

"No worries, sexy. I'm sure it was an accident."

I purposely wore a shirt two sizes too small, and his eyes were glued to my chest.

"Yeah, but . . . " I pointed at his shirt. "It's all over you."

"I could always take it off," he suggested with a wink.

I giggled. He was like putty in my hands and I noticed he was a lot closer than a few seconds before. His eyes were now checking out the rest of me.

Alexander licked his lips and touched my waist, gliding a finger over my exposed tattoo of a dragon with grayish-blue eyes, holding a sword in between its teeth.

"That's an intriguing dragon. What made you get it?"

"I like to slay people," I responded innocently.

He laughed, and like most people, took my answer as a joke.

"Cute," he said. "But I think you've got it wrong. In the stories, people slay the dragon, not the other way around."

"Well, in my version, the dragon is pissed, and she is getting revenge on everyone that has wronged her."

"A girl with imagination, I like that."

"And a shirtless Alexander. I'd like that," I said while stumbling a little.

He caught me in my pretend tipsy topple and seemed taken aback.

"You know my name, but I don't know yours."

"That's because everyone knows the famous Alexander. I'm merely a freshman hoping to make some new friends."

I gave him an angelic smile.

"You look familiar. Have we met before?"

I shook my head. I wasn't worried about him recognizing that I looked like Clara. We were twins, but we weren't identical. She wore glasses, had higher cheekbones, different colored eyes and hair.

"You want to go somewhere and talk? I mean, I do need to get out of this shirt."

"I don't know," I said, looking around. "That's a

tempting invitation, but I'm here with a friend, and I don't want her to worry."

"I'm sure your friend won't mind, plus I'll keep you safe."

I hesitated a little longer, and he attempted to seal the deal.

"You did spill your drink all over me. The least you could do is give me a little company while I get cleaned up."

I danced on the inside, pleased with how easy this was.

"I guess so," I shrugged.

He led me into a room upstairs at the end of the hallway and closed the door. I stood beside a large window that had no curtains, and could see out onto the busy street. Kids had flooded the street not the least bit concerned with the disturbance they were bringing to surrounding neighbors. Alexander went over to a dresser and pulled out a new shirt and pair of shorts.

I looked around, genuinely impressed. Assuming this was his room, there were a lot of awards in here.

"You never told me your name," he said.

"Tara," I lied.

"Alright, Tara, what brings you to this University?"

"I'd like to be a pediatrician."

"That's a good field. Are you from this area?"

At this point, he was still standing beside the dresser, watching me. I looked up at him and then quickly down again.

"No."

I keep my mannerisms appropriate for the role I was playing. I needed him to think I was shy, unsure of myself, and mesmerized by the opportunity to be alone with him.

"Why are you so quiet, Tara?"

He walked over to a mini-fridge and pulled out two drinks in unmarked plastic bottles.

Hmm, I'll bet those are his liquid rape accessories.

I smiled a little and tucked my long wavy hair behind one ear.

"You make me a little nervous."

Evidence of the pleasure he took in that response was written all over his face. He removed his shirt and smiled, revealing the picture-perfect chest that you would expect to see on the school's Mr. Popular. He offered me one of the bottles and I took it.

"Why do I make you nervous?"

I walked across the room, placed the bottle on the nightstand and sat on the bed. I'm done giving boosts to his ego. It was time to get this show on the road.

He came over, still shirtless, and sat down way too close to me. He put his hand on the back of my shoulder and rubbed small circles, and I said nothing.

"You aren't going to have a drink with me?" he asked.

"Sorry. I'm a little dizzy. I've probably already had too much to drink."

"I know something that might make you feel better."

"You do?" I asked.

He tossed his bottle onto the bed and then kissed me full on the lips. After a few seconds, I pulled away. Honestly, slightly stunned. There was no way he could fall into my trap this easily.

"I thought you only wanted to talk, Alexander?"

"Talking is one of the things I'd like to do."

He went in for another kiss, and I leaned back.

"I'm not that kind of girl."

"Come on, Tara. There's nothing wrong with a little kiss."

He tried again. I slapped him and then attempted to stand, but he grabbed my wrist.

"Let me go."

"Stop being so uptight."

"I think I've given you the wrong idea."

"You come to a party dressed like that, agree to come to a room with me, and now that you get the attention you want, you think you're going to walk away?"

He was getting angry, which was good. Angry people made mistakes, and they were less likely to notice things.

Yanking my arm out of his hold, I headed to the door, and he immediately blocked my exit.

Trying to push past him must have given him the ammunition he needed to use more force. Within seconds I'm on the bed, fighting (or pretending to) and yelling for him to get off of me.

The music from the party was blaring so loud my protests were being drowned out. Alexander was stronger than me and very heavy, which meant I had to do this just right.

He was pulling his shorts off now, calling me a bitch and a tease. He stuck his hand up my skirt and yanked down my underwear. I continued to squirm and quickly snapped my legs shut, hoping he wouldn't notice the sudden change in texture from my skin to the tape wrapped around my thighs. He didn't, and I breathed a sigh of relief.

Forcing my legs open again, he made some threat that I barely heard. Concentration was key at this point. Once he positioned his body in between my thighs, I pulled him close, locking my arms and legs around him as tight as I could.

His expected screams were like music to my ears. He tried to break my hold on him, but I hugged him closer. That was something I learned in my self-defense class. When you are locked on to your attacker, it's more difficult for them to punch, slap or kick you.

He struggled harder, and I waited a moment before

releasing my grip and, using the force of his pushing away to perfectly time a kick that knocked him to the floor.

"What the . . . fuck did you . . . do to me?"

Before I responded, I gave Alexander a kick in the side, and he screamed again. Grabbing my underwear and pulling them back on, I looked down at him.

He was in severe pain, and he should be. Razor blades can cut deep. He was the first to experience what I liked to call my 'thigh-high cutters'.

You see, I loved inventing cool things to aid me with my . . . self-protection. With this one, I took a thick foam cushion from an old bike seat and sliced it in half to make two thinner pieces.

Then I buried tons of tiny razor blades with the sharp side facing out, deep enough not to protrude unless pressure was applied. Next, I taped the edges of the pads to my inner upper thighs, and I was ready to party.

The room was dim, but I could see blood spilling onto the floor. I still couldn't believe my gadget worked so well. I should have it patented. Anyway, I didn't think Alexander's injuries were life-threatening, but he may be hurt for a while. Good.

"Mr. Wright," I said, placing a foot on one of his injured sides and pressing down. I tried to avoid getting more blood on my shoe than necessary. "Haven't you heard that no means no?"

He yelled and tried to wither away, and I kicked him again.

"You . . . fucking . . . bitch . . . you will not get away . . . with this."

I leaned down, pressed a finger into one of his cuts, and warm liquid drizzled out. I tasted it and felt a familiar tingle between my legs. Now, this was a turn-on—the victory over bringing down a soulless piece of shit was incomparable. I would have killed him, but Clara would not let me hear the end of it.

I patted the top of his head.

"Better save your breath. How else will you call for help?"

He grabbed my arm, but I easily tore it away. There was a small puddle of blood forming underneath him.

Would you look at that? Maybe, it was life-threatening after all.

I turned to leave, and once my hand touched the knob, a thought occurred to me. Clara and I may have been day and night regarding a lot of things, but we did share a love for reading. And the last book I finished was, The Scarlet Letter. This whole scenario was too perfect, and I couldn't resist.

I walked back to Alexander. He was still grunting and swearing at me. I rolled my eyes, damn he was dramatic. I squatted down and placed my hand under my skirt.

"What.... the fuck are you.... doing?" he said, trying to sit up, but failing.

I slid my underwear to the side, located the string for my tampon, gave it a pull, and it ejected smoothly.

I turned the open side down and placed a knee on Alexander's chest. He grabbed my wrist, halting me, and I pressed down harder on his wounded side. He instantly let go and started pushing at my knee.

I traced the letter 'A' on to his forehead using the tampon as a pen and my blood as the ink. He was moving so much it was hard to get it straight. It looked more like three squiggly lines with their own agenda than it did the letter 'A', but it would have to do.

I'd never seen a person get so angry.

"I'm going to . . . kill you." He reached for me again, and I quickly moved back.

"What . . . did you put . . . on me?"

"Only the letter A," I replied casually.

I could see the rage and confusion on his face as I stood.

Before exiting the room, I said over my shoulder, "In the book, it stood for adulterer. In this case, it can stand for asshole. Take your pick."

CHAPTER TWO

"PEOPLE CAN KISS MY ASS!"

"Where were you last night?" Clara asked.

I turned over and popped one eye open. She was standing in the living room wearing the pink and white bunny slippers that we shared. They were super comfy, and even though they were due to be replaced some time ago, we still kept them around.

I glanced at the clock. It's 3:45 pm, my usual time for rejoining the world. I guess the blackout I had last night, after my excitement with Alexander, didn't interfere with my normal wakeup schedule.

"It's 3:45, Clara. Are you just now getting up?"

"No, I had classes this morning. Then I came home and did some studying. Don't dodge the question."

I sat up on the couch that had become my permanent bed and gave her a grin.

"You know me? Shooting the breeze and bringing bad guys to their knees."

I said it in a singsong voice, adding two air pistols to imitate some cheesy 1970's cop show.

"Sidney. I'm serious. What were you up to? Did you have another blackout?"

"No, I did not have another blackout," I lied.

The blackouts were a problem I'd been having for a while now. For the most part, there was no rhyme or reason to them, but I noticed they occurred after I did something vengefully creative towards someone.

"The reason I wasn't home was that I had to work late."

Her eyes narrowed.

"Why don't I believe you?"

I got up from the couch and headed for the kitchen. A cup of juice would be fantastic right now.

"Because you always think I'm up to something. That's not news."

"That's because you *are* always up to something."

I opened the cabinet, got a glass, and poured myself a cup. I took a sip and closed my eyes. I loved orange juice.

Clara was watching me, willing me to reveal my actions from the night before. I would not volunteer any information. It wasn't that I didn't trust her; she just stressed too much. Clara waited until I sat down at our tiny two-seater kitchen table before speaking again.

"This morning in class, there was a lot of conversation about a wild party last night."

"Ooh, a college party. What's the world coming to?"

Clara continued, ignoring my sarcastic comment.

"The whispers around campus are that someone went crazy on Alexander Wright. You wouldn't know anything about that, would you?"

"I wouldn't."

She gave me a look. Not just any look, the look that a mother does when they know their child is lying. Proof that being born one minute earlier went straight to her head.

"Did you forget that I'm your twin and know when you're lying? Your thoughts are my thoughts, remember?"

"Umm, Clara, I don't think it works that way."

"It does with us. Now spill."

"Maybe he pissed the wrong person off. Ever think of that?"

"If that were the case, I'd be overjoyed, but as much as I want Alexander to pay for what he did, I don't want you going down with him. Were you at least careful?"

"No one saw me leave the room."

"Dammit, Sidney! I knew you did something."

Clara began pacing the floor, twirling her shoulder length reddish-brown hair and hyperventilating. I continued to sip my juice.

"This is bad. This is really bad. What if he sues? Wants retaliation? Comes looking for you? Recognizes you on the street? Or that you're my sister? I'm going to get expelled. I'll never be a pediatrician or anything for that matter. I'm ruined."

I waited patiently until her rant was over.

"People as bold as me rarely run into others on their level. You worry too much," I said.

"And you don't worry enough. Just because something rarely happens doesn't mean it can't happen. People are strange, cruel, and mean. It's best not to start trouble."

"People can kiss my ass."

"Sidney! You can't go about life, ignoring that there can be consequences to your actions."

I mulled over her stance on the matter and came to a one-word conclusion, nope. There was no room for regret about what I did to Alexander, but I hated seeing Clara upset. Nevertheless, if I could do it all over again, I would have shoved the tampon into his hole instead of back into mine.

"I know that, Clara."

She came and stood beside me.

"I'm worried about you, and it's not safe to do such impulsive things. Maybe you should talk to Barbara."

Not this again.

Barbara was Clara's one and only friend. She was a psychology major and acted like she was already fully licensed. Attempting to apply her premature skills to the 'why's' and 'how's' of Clara and I irked me.

Barbara knew we had a neglectful and abusive childhood and saw us as lab rats. Clara said she genuinely cared and that her advice had been helpful, but I thought she was nosy and a waste of time.

"Barbara is your friend, not mine."

"You should give her a chance. She's understanding, and you can trust her."

I finished my juice and studied my fingernails. Hot pink would be such a sexy color. Clara knew I had checked out of the conversation, so she said something certain to pull me back in.

"Sidney. Remember Darcy Lumbers and Mr. Strought?"

I looked up. Those were names I hadn't heard in a while. Darcy Lumbers, also known as the first person I killed, was the neighbor next door from my grandma.

When I was 17, she overheard me having a private conversation with Clara about how I had caught the pastor of our church cheating on his wife, and I was blackmailing him to give me money and pay for grandma's medical bills.

Ms. Lumbars should have minded her own business, but she refused. Her plan was to tell my grandmother what I was up to as soon as she saw her the next day. Admittedly, I was terrified, but there was no reason to worry.

The frail old woman didn't even make it to the next morning. She died sometime that night from an insulin overdose.

I was consumed by sadness and tears when I told the cops that my precious neighbor had been forgetting things for some time now. I guess she simply gave herself too much.

Mr. Strought was the previous landlord for this building. His death was ruled an accident after he took a fall down the stairs.

The split-second decision to end his life wasn't one I took lightly. Contrary to Clara's opinion, I was not incautious and preferred to stay away from such extremes, but I had no choice with him.

After letting himself into our apartment and rummaging through our things, he'd learned my secret and threatened to tell everyone if I didn't pay him more money. I begged and pleaded, but he couldn't be reasoned with.

He stormed out of the apartment with the lingering threat that I had one week to get him more money or else. I chose the or else option and gave him a shove down the stairs. Hey, it's not my fault his neck couldn't handle the tumble.

Anyway, after the police came to question everyone in the building, simple protocol, by the way, Clara lost her shit. I could barely calm her down, and she was so convinced that someone would find out what I did and come to arrest me that she didn't sleep for 48 hours. I, on the other hand, slept like a baby.

"I won't speak to Barbara, but I will consider moving."

"You've been talking about moving for months now. We can't simply run away from our problems, Sidney. I have school, and you have your bartending job."

"I could find a new job. Plus, this apartment is too small."

I motioned around our one-bedroom apartment. We'd

lived here for over a year now, and I was ready for something different.

"It's too small because you sleep on a couch and there are literally boxes of stuff everywhere. What happened to us sharing a room?"

"I can't fit in there with all your nightmares and middle-of-the-night crying episodes, Clara."

"Seriously?! I'm not that bad."

"And thunderstorms aren't that loud," I said, rolling my eyes with a slight smile.

"Fine. Stay out here on the lumpy couch, see if I care."

"I will," I responded unbothered.

"You know what I don't get? Why is it that I have nightmares and you don't?"

"Because I project my anger while you bottle yours up inside."

Clara seemed impressed with my response.

"See. I listened to Barbara that one time."

Clara shook her head and laughed a little. I could tell it lightened the mood, and I was thankful for that.

"I'm glad you listened, but that's not the point, and you know it. Wherever we are, you still have to reign in your reactions. If you're going to act the same way somewhere new. Why should we move?"

Ugh, I hated it when she got all logical with me. I was a free spirit, a thrill-seeker, and I didn't like to worry about consequences and repercussions. They were such a damper on life, and it was already too short as is.

"I'll consider talking to Barbara," I said, giving her the answer I knew she wanted.

"Good. Now that that matter is over. What are you doing today?"

"Not sure."

"You aren't visiting grandma?"

"Not today, maybe next week."

"You know she worries when we don't check-in?"

"Didn't you call her last week?"

"I did but—"

"Okay, we're good then."

Clara was about to protest when we heard a loud crash followed by a scream. Clara jumped and looked over at the wall that separated us from the people next door.

"I'm sorry, Marcus, I won't do it again," we heard a woman plead through the wall.

It was Shelly, a poor girl whose part-time job seemed to be, being her boyfriend Marcus' punching bag. His booming voice echoed through the walls of our apartment, pulling us into the violence and destruction we wanted no part of.

I like to give the pain, not witness it, and Marcus was raining on my parade for the second time that week, bullying his girlfriend. I took a deep breath and released it.

Not my business. Not my business. I mentally chanted to myself.

Marcus was 35, and Shelly was 19. I think she had been with him since 16, and the man continuously stayed angry about something.

It was always hard for me to understand why Shelly stayed with him. He beat her black and blue more times than I could count, forced her to sell her body to pay rent, and even made her sleep in the hallway or on the sidewalk as punishment several times.

That was only counting the things that I saw. If he did all that with the world as a witness, I would hate to know what he did to her behind closed doors.

The handful of times I talked to her, she always seemed so nice. The story of how she wound up with Marcus was the typical tale you would expect.

A naive young girl, kicked out of her parent's house way too soon, scared and searching for love in all the wrong places. The bad guy enters the scene and uses her vulnerabilities against her.

In one of my brief conversations with Shelly, I told her that last I checked, love didn't crack your ribs, repeatedly send you to the emergency room, or strike you so hard you don't wake up until the next day.

Her response was to shrug and say that sometimes it was her fault for making him so angry. I stopped listening at that point. Victims often blamed themselves, Clara did that sometimes, too, and I hated it. In the end, I wished Shelly well and learned to limit our conversations.

Another bang of something hitting the wall and Shelly crying out caused me to mentally locate where I hid my gun. Clara would freak if she knew I had one, but what she didn't know wouldn't hurt her.

I hoped like hell, Marcus wasn't making a Shelly-sized hole in the wall. The repair time would take forever since the maintenance team in this building was nonexistent.

Clara removed her glasses, squeezed her eyes shut and covered her face. She's thinner than me, but I'm an inch taller. I always joke that the difference in our height is from her cowering so much.

She liked my sense of humor most of the time, and knew that I would never intentionally hurt her.

I hated seeing her scared or upset. It gave me the need to react and fix it, much like how I felt right now. I could see her trembling, and all I wanted to do was hug her, but I knew, for reasons I won't get into right now, that was not a good idea.

Her eyes opened, and the bluish gray color looked weaker somehow. Clara's eyes were truly the window to her soul, and I could always tell when something was wrong.

My eyes were dark gray, and they didn't tell you shit about my soul that I didn't want them to.

I always wondered who exactly we got our eyes from. Our mom was black with dark brown eyes, and we never knew our dad.

Mom said it's some guy in Vegas she had a one-night stand with, then later, she claimed it was a man who owned a gas station in Nebraska. I'd love the truth, but the woman lied so much, I doubted I'd ever figure it out.

"I can't listen to this anymore. I'm going to my room to study and turn on some music," Clara announced.

"I agree with you there," I said, going to grab my black backpack. After unzipping it, I spotted a few white sheets of paper stapled together and pulled them out. It was an exam with a 98% on it.

"Clara, did you use my backpack again?"

"Sorry I couldn't find mine."

"It's cool, it's not like I use it much, anyway. Congratulations on getting another A, you deserve it. You studied so much for this test I feel like I also learned everything about HIPAA compliance."

"Thanks. Where are you going?"

"To the park. You want to come?"

"No."

I knew she would say that. Clara hardly ever left the apartment. When she did, it was either for school or to visit our grandmother.

I've been trying to no avail to get her to visit me down at the bar. But the girl was terrified of being out too often. She was the same when we were younger—only making herself known when it came to school and other necessary outings.

I pulled the backpack on and located my shoes.

"You know when you graduate, you actually have to leave the house to work as a pediatrician, right?"

Another yell penetrates through the wall, and I watched Clara desperately try to hold it together. I knew the abuse from our childhood was making this neighborly episode of violence that much worse for her. She gave me a tiny smile.

"I know that. Don't worry about me. I'm getting better with my anxieties and fears. Barbara has been a saint helping me learn to cope. When it's my time, I'll be ready."

"Yeah, right. You're going to stay in hiding for the rest of our lives."

"I will not. You just wait. I'm going to be doing all sorts of things and living my best life. There will be no more room for you and your sarcastic comments."

"I'll believe it when I see it. Until then, I'm going to the park. Enjoy your view of the four walls."

She stuck her tongue out at me and rushed to the bedroom.

I sing a song in my head as I pass the apartment where Marcus is still currently beating the shit out of poor Shelly. It was sad no one in the building tried to help anymore.

A few residents did intervene in the past, but she always returned to Marcus or bailed him out of jail. The girl is either stuck on stupid or so broken she couldn't be fixed.

Whatever the reason, it has lost her pity from most of us that live here. I think Clara was the only one who still felt horrible for the girl, but since Clara hardly ever left the apartment, Shelly wouldn't be getting rescued anytime soon.

Once I made it downstairs I spotted Gary, a sixteen-year-old delinquent that lived in apartment 3 with his alcoholic father. He was obsessed with fire and a real danger to the building.

The fire department had already put out two small mysterious fires here. No one ever saw anything suspicious, but I put my money on Gary being guilty. At the moment, he was playing with a lighter in the corner, staring at the flames in true wonderment.

I, of all people, understood out-of-the-ordinary obsessions, but do it in private and only harm your intended victims, not everybody!

He momentarily tore his eyes away from the glow of the flame and glanced at me, "Hey Sidney, you're looking good today."

"Find a new hobby, Gary," I said as I continued walking towards the exit.

Before I made it outside, I saw Mr. Gregory, the resident in apartment 1, struggling to get inside. He was a sweet older gentleman that I pegged to be in his late 70's. He never had much family coming around, so Clara and I checked on him when we could.

"Hi Mr. Gregory. Do you need some help getting inside your apartment?"

"Please," he responded with a shaky voice. "This damn arthritis is ruining my fingers."

I took the key from his hand, unlocked the door, and then helped him inside to his favorite chair by the TV.

"Thanks, Clara, you are such a sweetheart," he said, looking up over thick clear-framed glasses. Would you like something to drink before you go?"

I smiled. He truly was precious, and halfway senile too.

"Mr. Gregory, it's Sidney, not Clara."

He squinted at me.

"Ahh, Sidney, I see it now. I always confuse the two of you. I saw Clara yesterday morning on her way to school, and she brought me my mail. You two are so kind. Your parents certainly did raise you right," he said, nodding his head.

I wasn't sure if he was doing that to agree with his own assumption or it was some nerve problem. I placed his keys on the table next to him and passed him the remote.

"I better get going. Do you need anything before I leave?"

“Nothing I can think of. Then again, my memory is so bad I will likely remember once you are gone."

I patted his hand gently.

“Don't worry, I will try to stop by a little later, and if I don’t, Clara probably will tomorrow."

He thanked me again, and I let myself out of the apartment. On my way out the door, I noticed two crisp twenty dollar bills on a desk.

Under normal circumstances I would help myself to one of them, but Mr. Gregory had been nothing but kind to me. I didn’t need to steal from him. I did enough of that at my job.

I crossed the street and began the seven-minute walk to the park. The day was overcast, but the temperature was perfect. I should be able to read a couple of chapters of this amazing psychological thriller that I picked up last week before it's time to head to work.

I thought back to Mr. Gregory and smiled. I wasn't an asshole all the time. As a matter of fact, I enjoyed being nice to people when they deserved it. The acts of kindness made me feel purer and closer to Clara. She only saw the good in others, and that gave me hope. Maybe I could start seeing it too.

I made it inside the parameters of the park and spotted my favorite bench near the giant oak tree. It was empty and waiting for me. As I moved towards it with a pep in my step and a smile in my heart, I was caught off guard by the sudden mushiness under my foot.

I stopped walking, but didn't look down. I could feel my previously serene vibe being replaced by indignation.

Without looking down, I was positive I'd just stepped in dog shit. I HATED dog shit, probably as much as I hated the owners who felt no responsibility to pick it up.

It was not my job to clean up behind them. This was not a group task; I didn't want a fucking pet. I stepped off the paved walking path and into the grassy area, sliding my shoe over the lush greenery. Yup, it was feces. Thick, brown, and gooey.

It was likely Mrs. Larks's dog, Bella. Mrs. Larks lived somewhere in the area and loved bringing her dog to the park. I didn't know the woman personally.

I simply overheard numerous conversations from other park guests complaining about her allowing Bella to use the park grounds as a restroom. Then, walking away like the park could flush the mess itself.

After cleaning my shoe as best as I could, I walked the rest of the way to the bench urging myself to calm down. I purchased these shoes two weeks ago and they were expensive. Now, they were practically worthless. My vision momentarily blurred and my shoulders tensed.

"Murder is not mandatory. Murder is not mandatory," I repeated to myself.

Besides, there was nothing I could do right now, no need to let it ruin the rest of my day. I reluctantly tabled the matter and plopped down onto the bench. It welcomed my presence with a gentle creak.

I pulled out my book and began to read, stopping a few times to watch the kids playing and laughing. Three of them were on the swing set, and another four were playing a game of tag. I never played tag as a kid.

The most fun I had during childhood was that one-time grandma sent Clara and me to camp. It was a unique experience and a real treat. That was until the accident happened with Selena Higgins. Poor Selena, she couldn't keep her opinions to herself.

I looked back down at my book. I'd made it through a whole chapter, and the killer was closing in on his victim. I hoped he got her; she was so annoying. I readjusted in my seat to get comfortable.

The fate of the fictional girl was just about to be uncovered when someone approached from behind and placed their hands over my eyes.

CHAPTER THREE

"I EXITED MY KILLER TRANCE."

"Hi gorgeous," the slightly deep male voice said from behind me.

"Hi Nathan," I replied in a flirty tone.

He removed his hand from over my eyes and came to sit down beside me on the bench. He was so adorable and nonthreatening. I loved that about him. To be clear, I didn't love him and probably never would, but he loved me, and that was enough.

I scooted closer to my boyfriend of a little over five months, and he took my hand in his and kissed it.

He was such a gentleman. I met him when he came into the bar one night and defended me by punching out a guy that had gotten a little too handsy. I mean, I would have handled him myself, but Nathan's route was less messy.

"You didn't even jump. Were you expecting someone else?" he asked, pretending to be hurt.

"Of course not. I'm just not very jumpy, I guess."

"You're a strange woman, Sidney Jacobson."

He had no idea.

I spent eight months training myself not to panic so easily. In order to do this, I poked a hole into the edge of a slightly damp rag and then attached it to a giant timer that had a protruding dial with a small hook on the end.

Every night, I placed the timer on the table next to the couch and slept with the top of my head touching it.

When the timer went off an hour later, not only did the blaring sound yank me from my sleep, the position of the dial caused the rag to fall partially onto my face.

My nerves weren't on board for that ride in the beginning, but eventually, I learned to wake without startling. The body is a miraculous thing. You simply have to train it.

"My strangeness is why you like me," I said.

"You're right," he replied, kissing me again, this time on the lips. "I went by your place to surprise you."

"Aww that's sweet. Did Clara tell you I was here?"

"No. Actually, no one answered. I could hear music playing though."

"Yeah, she probably didn't hear the door."

He agreed, but sounded unsure of something.

"Either way, I decided to check here in case you were hanging out at your favorite place."

"It is my favorite place. When I'm not with you, of course."

He smiled and then looked serious.

Uh oh.

"Sidney?" He said hesitantly, "Does Clara not like me?"

"Why do you say that?"

"Because she doesn't seem interested in meeting me."

"I told you Clara has a lot of . . . " I paused to find the right words, "wariness to new people, especially guys. You know how it was for us growing up."

"I do. That's why I want to make sure I wasn't putting her off in any way."

"Trust me, it's not you. And today she was trying to drown out the horrific sounds of the neighbors."

"I didn't hear any commotion in the building when I was there."

I shrugged.

"Maybe Marcus had knocked Shelly unconscious."

"Damn. That's horrible. Those two were fighting again?"

"If you mean he was throwing the punches, and she was catching them, then, yeah, they were fighting."

"Sidney, I know you're only being sarcastic because living in the midst of all that makes you nervous. It's okay to tell me you're afraid."

I batted my eyelashes and once again, played the role. Being a damsel in distress was such a tiring job. He picked up my hand and cradled it in his.

"Baby, my offer still stands."

I nodded. Cutesy names from him I could get with. I looked down at our hands, his was protectively covering mine. Nathan wanted me to move in with him, but that was a big fat no.

Nathan didn't know my secret, only three people did and as far as my vengeful extracurricular activities went... it would be much harder to hide them with him constantly in my personal space.

If I got the itch to kill someone, how in the hell would I scratch it? I couldn't exactly come home covered in blood and expect him not to pry.

Therefore, I declined his invitation by stating that I couldn't leave Clara. He surprised me when he said she was welcome to come too, but I countered that it would never work because most men made Clara apprehensive.

"The answer is still no, Nathan." I said tenderly.

"If you ever change your mind, I'm here." He exhaled quietly and stared out at the playing kids before asking, "Do you have to work tonight?"

"Yeah, at eight. What about you? Selling gadgets today?"

Nathan worked as the manager at an electronics store.

He always brought me cool merchandise, such as wireless earpieces, retro handheld video games and TV headphones.

One time he even brought me a wearable voice changer. It's so cool, you pull the straps behind your ears, and a small, thin black square goes over your mouth.

"I'm off today. You want me to take you to work?"

A girl jogged by, and I looked up at her. She had nice form and such a cute workout jumpsuit. I loved those things. Being stylish when working out is a must. I looked celebrity sexy every time I attended boxing class.

"Do you think she's cute?" I asked, nodding at the runner girl.

Nathan laughed, slightly uncomfortable with the question.

"I think you're cute," he said, pulling me closer to him.

"It won't bother me if you do," I said honestly.

"I didn't even look at her, Sidney. I was busy watching my own gorgeous girlfriend."

"Well, take a look now."

The girl was some distance away at this point.

"I can't see her face, and only a blur of her body. Why are you asking me this?"

"I'm just curious."

"Curious because you and I haven't had sex and you think other girls will steal my attention?"

"Curious because I want to know what you're into."

"I'm into you," he said, kissing me on the lips.

I take a moment to enjoy it. He was a good kisser, and I relished being close to him in this way, but ultimately the ride stopped here. I ended the kiss and stared into his eyes.

"That better be a given," I said in response to his playful comment.

He seemed to be sweating bullets, so I stopped pressing

him about the jogger girl. Besides, I'm not jealous. I knew that Nathan was only into me.

He put his arm around me, leaned back onto the bench, and closed his eyes. I checked the time, realizing I didn't have long before I needed to prepare for work.

I decided to take in a little more reading when I spotted an old lady and her dog entering the park.

Well, would you look at that?

It was the dog, Bella, and her bitch, Mrs. Larks.

"You alright, babe?" Nathan asked. "You suddenly got really stiff."

I shook my head and exited my killer trance.

"Everything's fine. I just remembered I might need to leave for work sooner than I thought."

He stood and offered me his hand. After sliding my book back into my bag I took it.

"No worries. I can take you back to your place to change for work and then drop you off."

"You're truly a lifesaver."

Nathan smiled, appreciating the comment, but not privy to my intent. He'd unknowingly saved Mrs. Larks from my wrath. I sighed as I forced my nerves to calm. I needed to learn to reign in my anger. Lately, it had been getting stronger.

My stance towards risk was becoming almost cavalier. Being reckless was the last thing I needed.

Especially since a few months ago, I began experiencing blackouts. I would wake up at home on the couch, not sure how I got there. Handicaps like that made me vulnerable.

Therefore, putting in an effort to keep my temper in check was wise.

Please don't misunderstand; none of this meant Mrs. Larks was in the clear. She and I would have a much-needed conversation.

The Lucky Glass Lounge already had a full crowd when I started my shift. I walked behind the counter and lifted my blue halter top, tying a knot on the side so that it showcased my waist, and tied my apron on. Then I pulled my hair up into a quick messy ponytail while a few guys watched me from their stools.

I could smell their drool from here. Such animals. I hoped their wallets are full.

I'd been bartending there for 12 months now. I used a fake ID and bar certification that an ex-con in my neighborhood made for me to uphold the lie that I was an experienced 25-year-old ready to tend the bar.

Thankfully, Grid, the bar owner, didn't do a full background check. Truthfully speaking, I think he was more concerned with how my looks could up his sales.

Fortunately for me, I'm a fast learner and picked up the recipe for several popular drinks on the first night.

Regardless, I never worked alone. There was always at least one other person running the show with me, and since I only worked from eight until midnight, it was necessary.

"Hey Cassie," I said to the bartender I'd be working with tonight. She was tall, super slim, with tattoos covering her arms and neck. She was very down-to-earth and obsessed with two things: a good party and a cute guy. I'd attended a few parties with her and each one was unforgettable.

"Little doll! How the hell are you?"

I laughed at her chosen nickname for me. It's pretty self-explanatory. Everyone thought I was small and cute. Story of my life.

"I think there was a sporting event tonight, and it's bringing in tons of traffic," Cassie said. "Are you ready to make some money?"

In response, I adjusted my shirt and shook my boobs. On nights like this, not only did I make great tips, I helped myself to a little extra from Grids cut.

"Hell yeah," I said with a grin.

Cassie wasn't kidding. People were coming in nonstop. The bar got so full at one point, a fight broke out because a guy got tired of customers yelling orders over his head and told the wrong patron to "Shut the fuck up."

Cassie and I watched the outpour of violence from behind the bar, placing bets and eating peanuts.

Unfortunately, the show ended fairly quickly. Grids security team was fantastic at their job, and as they dragged the two guys outside, I discreetly slid the third $50 bill into my pocket for the night.

"I need a Dark n' Stormy for the gentleman at the end of the bar," Cassie called out.

I had just placed two dirty martinis and a Long Island Iced Tea on the counter in front of three eager customers. I searched my brain for the recipe of Cassie's request.

"That's the one with the small splash of honey, right?"

She winked at me.

I prepared the drink and placed it in front of the guy. He grumbled a thanks, barely looking up. I didn't take it personally. Lots of people that frequented the lounge were sad, depressed, and overwhelmed with life.

A man put up his hand and I made my way over to him. I'd seen him here quite a few times before. I didn't know if he jumped from bar to bar, but every time I waited on him, he was already slightly drunk.

"What will you have tonight?"

"You, if you're on the menu."

He laughed a little too loud and then coughed. I waited until he finished hacking up a lung before saying, "I'm not, but Heineken is, and if you buy a full pitcher I'll think of you in my dreams."

The guy couldn't open his wallet fast enough. He obviously didn't possess a high level of intelligence.

"Well, start me a tab sweetie pie. I'm going to be all yours tonight."

He passed me his card, and I fisted it a little too tight, causing it to crack. I fucking hated pet names from slimy men. I turned to face the register and casually checked the card.

The crack was almost splitting it in two. However, if I was careful, I could keep it in one piece and hopefully give it back to him without him even noticing.

My plan went smoothly, and a couple of minutes later, he had his card, beer, and gross pickup lines to keep him company.

A woman took a seat at one of the newly vacated stools, and I walked over to collect her order. I had never seen her before, but she reminded me of Selena, the bully from the camp we went to as kids.

Wasn't I just thinking about her a few days ago?

Funny how when you think of something, other things occur to line up with those thoughts.

When we were ten, Clara and I were adopted by grandma Nancy. Understanding the horrific childhood we had already endured, she thought it would be helpful to give Clara and me some positive experiences and send us to camp.

However, it didn't turn out to be the exciting, innocent adventure she wished it to be. Come to think of it, it may have made things worse.

Most of the kids were nice, but Selena Higgins was not. She was twelve, had been attending the camp every summer since she was seven, and believed she ran the place.

A group of mindless wannabes followed her around while she made fun of the other kids and sucked up to the counselors to get out of doing things that she considered beneath her.

Selena didn't exactly bully me, but Clara was the perfect candidate for her torture.

After dealing with it for two weeks and getting no help from the counselors, I think I just snapped. I was tired of Clara and I being everyone's punching bag.

So one night, when Selena opted out of the activities because she wasn't feeling well, I visited her cabin. She was asleep, so I snuck around to the side window and quietly slid it open.

Earlier I had noticed a beehive in a tree nearby her cabin, so I used that along with a cool accordion-type tunnel that we crawled through for outside activities to work my plan. Even back then, I was super crafty.

I placed one end inside the window and the other over the beehive. It took a few shakes, but eventually, the hive came loose and rolled down my make-shift chute and into the cabin.

I quickly closed the window and got out of there, but not before I spared a look inside. Selena was still in her bed, sleeping peacefully, but the bees were angry. With their home disturbed, they were rapidly exiting the hive and filling the room.

I didn't get to see Selena before the paramedics took her away, but rumors suggest that her face looked like hamburger meat.

I snapped out of the memory and smiled at the woman my mind now labeled the adult version of Selena. Pre bee enhancements, of course.

"What can I get you?" I asked while wiping the area in front of her before sticking the rag back into my apron.

She looked up from her phone as if she didn't understand the question.

"My husband says he's leaving me because I'm too fat to be a wife. What drink pairs well with that?"

I guess I was on counselor duty tonight.

"I'm not sure of the drink, but a new husband would be a good start. There's plenty of available men here."

She gave me a weak smile.

"That's some advice I needed before I married him."

Her eyes were sad. I couldn't imagine my husband insulting me like that and then living to see another day. But hey, everyone wasn't like me.

"Give me a second. I have something you might like," I said.

I made her a Very Pink Raspberry Cosmopolitan and added a colorful straw. If anyone needed some cheery colors in their life, it was this woman. I took it back to her and placed it on the bar.

Her previous weak smile lifted a little higher.

"Festive."

"It's called a Very Pink Raspberry Cosmopolitan, and it's on the house."

I figured I could throw her a bone. I had pocketed a decent amount of money tonight, and I was in a good mood.

"It is very pink." She looked up at me. "Thanks."

I patted her hand and moved on to the next customer.

When midnight arrived, my shift ended, and I was beat. I said goodnight to Cassie, clocked out, and headed home. The lounge would be open for another two hours, but I rarely stayed until closing. Mainly because I didn't need to. The hourly wage, tips, and bonuses I took for myself were more than enough compensation.

Instead of calling an Uber, as any normal person would at midnight in a sometimes questionable neighborhood, I opted to walk home. I didn't live too far away, and the quiet was calming.

It also gave me time to deposit my cash into the ATM, which I did every night after work. I wasn't worried about being harassed because I was a pretty good fighter, and I always had my razor blade with me.

It's small, inconspicuous, and I kept it in my mouth.

I had no idea something like that was possible, but imagine my joy when a woman I met at the bar one night pulled hers out to brag.

My interest was piqued, and the kind lady explained how she did it. It's all about size and how well you cover it to protect your mouth. Some people didn't mind having the blade in their mouth unprotected, but others covered it.

I opted to cover mine as well. I used a small piece of hard plastic to ensure I didn't cut my gums, and so far, I hadn't suffered any problems.

Even the risk of swallowing it isn't as high as you'd think because I'd fallen asleep with it in my mouth a few times. It scared Clara so bad she told me she'd rather I carried a gun, and that's saying something.

I decided that wasn't the best time to let her know that I had a gun as well. I had stolen it from a security guy one night that was drunk off his ass. I kept it at the bottom of a container where I stored my clothes.

Coming up on the side of my building, I ran into Joe Harvey. Everyone called him Joho.

He was the homeless guy that had made the alley area his home. Joho would literally screw anything if the impulse arose, hence the 'Ho' part of his name.

He was grinning and holding his penis. He was always holding his penis.

"You and I could have a good time," he said to me through teeth so black they were practically invisible in the darkness. The streetlight about 20 feet away was doing a poor job of illuminating the pathway.

"Fuck off, Joho."

I'd never met anyone more sex-obsessed than Joho. I'd passed through this area many nights and witnessed him fucking everyone from homeless women, to homeless men, to himself when no one else was available.

The rumors around the neighborhood were that some lab experimented on him, then dumped him back off into civilization.

I've considered putting him out of his misery, but every time I remind myself that murder is not mandatory.

Joho shrugged and walked over to the side of the building, and began dragging his dick against the brick wall. Now that made me take a pause. I watched him, realizing that his next action could easily top the bar fight.

There was a hole, dugout in between two bricks. I gave myself one guess as to how it got there. Joho put his dick in the hole, and started pumping away.

I stared in amazement.

Didn't that hurt?

From the looks of it, he wasn't feeling any pain, and if he was, it must have sped up the process because a few thrusts later he came in a rush, and semen splattered the wall. I was stuck between wanting to vomit or giving him applause.

Fuck that bar fight; this was the highlight of my night.

Chapter Four

"I LOVE A GOOD FIGHT."

The next day I woke up around my usual 3:45-4 pm slot.

Clara was at the table studying. She was wearing a pajama set covered in Mini Mouse faces. She was always fully clothed. No shorts, no skirts, and no tank tops.

That scandalous style was all me. Her brows were dented as she stared and mouthed the words to what she was reading. I suspected it was more about hospital protocols. That's what they were working on last week.

I was so proud of her, and I thought it was incredible that she wanted to help kids. Then again, considering our childhood, it added up. Sometimes people liked to do for others what wasn't done for them.

We weren't protected very well and learned way too early that the monster in the closet is the same one you're forced to call Uncle.

I stretched and went to the bathroom to brush my teeth and wash my face. When I returned, Clara had moved from the table to the couch.

Oh Shit.

"What Clara?"

"I saw Alexander. He was on crutches limping around campus. What did you do to him, Sidney?"

"I thought we were over this."

"We were, but you never told me what you did. Honestly, I didn't care, but now I want to know."

"I think you already know what I did."

"You love your mind games, don't you?"

In reply, I shrugged and found a new shirt to put on. The one I slept in had a rip in it. Opening the box beside the couch where I kept my clothes, I noticed there were only three clean ones left.

Wash day needs to happen sooner rather than later. I should also do some shopping. I saw a cute pair of red heels that were calling my name and I would like some more skirts.

"Are you washing clothes soon?" I asked, holding up my shirt.

Clara rolled her eyes.

"Fine Sidney! I'll take a guess. Does it have anything to do with that contraption you were making with the razor blades and cushions?"

"And you say I'm the one that likes to play mind games."

I tossed my old shirt on the floor and pulled the new one on. It was a yellow tank top with the words, 'I shine brighter than you' written across the front in bold pink letters.

"You told me you were making something to slice boxes open faster and safer at the bar!"

"And you believed me? I could have simply used a box cutter, Clara."

"No I didn't believe you, but I didn't want to ask. Trust me. I'm happy Alexander got what was coming to him, he is scum, but if I lose you, I don't know what I'll do. I can't exist without you."

"Clara, don't worry. Nothing is going to happen to me."

I vaguely wondered if that was a lie. I was living life quite perilously these days.

"I'll stop worrying when you stop doing dangerous things. Remember, you are supposed to be working on being nice and letting things go."

"Playing nice is your thing."

Clara exhaled and sat down next to me. This was her way of waving the white flag or trying to come at things from another angle. I think she believed it made me more acceptable to her suggestions and more willing to answer questions. She admired my hot pink nail polish.

"That looks nice. When did you do it?"

"When I got home from the bar last night." I turned to her, suddenly remembering the details of the night before. "Oh shit. I didn't tell you I saw Joho outside fucking the brick wall?"

Clara giggled and her eyes got wide.

"You didn't!"

"Yes, I did."

"Gross! Did you run away? I would have been mortified."

"Hell no. I watched the show all the way up until he creamed the wall."

"That's repulsive. I could never do that."

"It was very entertaining. You should try watching him some time merely to see what happens next."

Clara's face twisted in disgust.

"Eww, no thank you. That's an image I don't need."

She shook as if the physical act could somehow remove the invading thoughts.

"Are you going to see grandma today?" she asked.

"Yes, Clara, you can stop hounding me. I'm finally going to check on grandma today. I'm also going to my boxing class. What are your plans?"

Clara sighed.

"The usual. Study and sleep."

"No Barbara?"

"I'll see her tomorrow."

My poor sister was always avoiding the world. I guess some people were only here to look after others. I shook my head at her.

"Speaking of your limited social life. Nathan thinks you don't like him."

"What!? I love Nathan. I think he's great for you."

"Yeah, but you only know that through what I tell you. He thinks that means you aren't a fan."

"I know Nathan is a good guy. He gives off that vibe. Plus you wouldn't be with him if he weren't. And as far as meeting him . . . ultimately that is your call, not mine. He's your boyfriend."

She made a good point.

"He can meet you when the time is right."

Clara smiled in agreement.

I caught the bus to get to my grandma's house. One day I was seriously going to consider buying a car. Public transportation was tolerable, but the peace and quiet I would get in a car would be hard to beat.

I finally arrived at grandma's place and climbed the three stairs that landed me in front of her apartment door. I knocked, and within a matter of seconds, the door was opened, and I was staring into the face of one of the most angelic women on earth.

Giving me a once over, then lifting a brow at my too short shorts, tennis shoes, and tank top, a proud smile covered her face, and she opened her arms to me.

"Sidney, baby I'm so glad you've come. How are you?"

"I'm wonderful, grandma. How about you?"

"Better now that you're here. Come in, come in."

I entered the apartment, and I was immediately met with the familiar smell of baked cookies. Grandma loved baking.

Even though she couldn't eat most of the sweet treats she created due to her diabetes, she still enjoyed the hobby and passed it out to the neighborhood kids. I took a seat at the table, and she joined me, lowering herself down slowly.

"Are you alright?" I asked.

"I'm good, sweetie. Nothing for you to worry about. The older you get the slower you move that's all." She patted my hand. "Have you been taking care of yourself?"

"I promise I have."

She squinted her eyes at me like she didn't believe me. I had no idea why people thought I lied so much.

"You've been keeping your temper under control?"

Jeez! You get into a few fights as a kid, set a stuffed animal your mother gave you on fire, and get caught letting bees into a girl's cabin at camp, and suddenly you can't be trusted.

"Scout's honor Grandma," I said, giving her a salute, "I've been on my best behavior."

Okay, it made sense now. I guess I was always lying. But in my defense, I had to learn to be more careful and tell little white lies to protect those I care about. I assumed she decided my answer would suffice because she moved on.

"I've seen Clara, but I haven't seen you in a few weeks. What's been keeping you busy?"

"Working mostly. Did you get the money I sent for your doctor bills?"

"I did indeed. Thank you again. You always take such good care of me. What about school? How's that going?"

I studied her.

"I'm not the one in school, Grandma. That's Clara."

"Oh right. Forgive me, dear. It's hard to keep up sometimes."

"Are you sure you're okay?"

She gave me a tiny smile.

"I'm fine. It's you I worry about."

"Why's that?" I asked, tilting my head.

She began to say something but caught herself. Instead, she replaced her troubled expression with yet another cheerful smile.

"Would you like some cookies?"

"Always!"

She got up and brought me a plate with two chocolate chip cookies on it, and then headed to her bedroom. I immediately took a large bite. It was beyond delicious. So soft, gooey, and sweet. I tell her all the time she should enter contests.

Grandma returned and placed a medium-sized bag on the table.

"What's this?" I asked through a mouth full of chocolate chips.

"It's a sweater I made for Clara. The last time I spoke with her, I told her I would finish it up so that she could have it."

"It looks nice," I said, peering into the bag.

Due to my cookie crumb covered fingers, I didn't want to touch it. Even still, I could see that it was a soft pink color that I knew Clara would love.

"Oh, I didn't forget about you. There is a box of fingernail polish with all those jewels and stuff you are into at the bottom."

"Aww thanks, Grandma."

I kissed her on the cheek. She was such a wonderful

woman. I loved her just as much as Clara and would do anything to protect her.

"You're most welcome. It's good to see you happy."

She watched me enjoying the cookie and then it happened. A slight sadness took over.

"Oh Sidney," she said, touching my face.

Uh-oh. The guilt was creeping into her eyes. I've told her repeatedly that she had no reason to feel bad.

Adopting us from the grips of our horrible childhood was the best thing she could have ever done. She wasn't even our blood relative, but she had and always will love us like her own.

"Grandma, you gave us love and protection when we needed it most. We are happy now because of you."

"I know, but I wish I could have done more or got to you sooner. Every time I see you I'm reminded of how special you are and how much damage that damn crazy family caused."

I took her hand in mine.

"I choose my own path. Don't worry about me. Even when you're not there, I have Clara remember? She's always with me."

Grandma only continued to smile at me. It was the same warm, understanding, non-judgmental smile from my childhood.

The smile of a kind next-door neighbor that my mom would pawn us off on when she'd prefer a night of partying, drugs, or fucking her brother, to being a loving mother.

Grandma witnessed a lot of what we went through and tried to shelter us, but even she couldn't protect us from my uncle Trevor's wandering hands in the night.

Luckily, when I was ten, my mother was sent to prison for killing a man in broad daylight. It didn't take much for her to sign over her parental rights to Grandma Nancy.

Fate is a funny thing.

It took my mother's freedom to be taken away for me to gain mine. I gave Grandma all the credit for bringing sunshine into my life. Now the only darkness in my world was the darkness that lived in me.

I punched the bag as hard as I could 20 times. One for each year that I'd been alive. I loved boxing. I first started taking classes when I was thirteen.

Grandma, and a child psychologist I had to see after the camp incident, believed it to be a great way to release my aggression.

There was a center not too far from the house that offered free boxing classes, so they set me up for my first day, and I fell in love.

Punching people for sport was right up my alley. True, they could punch me as well, but I loved a good fight.

I stepped back and took a second to clear my head. I was thinking about Mrs. Larks and how I wanted to wring her neck for ruining my shoes.

It was a good mental target, but I was starting to get upset, and I didn't like being upset when I couldn't do anything about it. I decided instead to think about people I'd already settled the score with.

Mr. Strought.

Punch

Ms. Lumbars

Punch, Punch

Alexander.

Punch, Punch, Punch.

Yes, that felt better. I was more in control and level-headed. I normally worked with a guy named Coleman.

He'd been helping me for the last few years with my form and ways to properly defend myself. Today was his day off, but I still enjoyed the personal practice.

I continued counting the blows in my head as they landed when I was suddenly interrupted.

"You have good form, but you favor your right side too much."

I stopped and turned around.

"Come again?" I said, trying to catch my breath.

"Your right side, you favor it too much. Being as small as you are you don't need to favor one side over the other. You need to be sure to take advantage of both."

I mentally rolled my eyes. I was going to play nice today, no outbursts.

"I'll keep that in mind," I said, facing away from her.

I wanted her to go away. I didn't like her tone. The bitch sounded like a know-it-all. Why would she immediately assume I favored one side over the other? Even if I did, there were better ways to start a conversation.

"I could teach you. I've been boxing for ten years now and I know a lot."

Dammit, she was still here.

"I'm sure you do, but no thanks."

"Tell you what. Let's get in the ring and I'll show you where your weaknesses are."

Was that a challenge? I loved challenges. Even if I wasn't more skilled, I bet I could outsmart her.

I faced her again, displaying the most hesitant expression I could find.

"Okay, but you have to take it easy on me. I am new at this."

"Oh honey, it shows," she cackled, swatting my shoulder.

I followed her to the squared circle, and we put on our

gear. The first few minutes I spent tossing out senseless and ill-timed jabs that didn't connect.

She hit me several times, pausing after each strike to inform me of what I did wrong and why I needed better focus.

I patiently waited, listening to her yammer as I analyzed and studied her style. I will give it to her. She was talented, but too cocky, which can ruin even the best of them.

When she 'caught' me with a side blow on my left for the third time in a row, I was finally ready to strike.

"You see," she said. "You are still not successfully blocking my hits. Now when I go this way, you should—"

I surprised her with a speedy four-punch combo. Right cross, left hook, right cross again and finalized it with a left uppercut that knocked her on her ass.

She was stunned and finally, for the first time since I'd met her, silent. Underestimating my craftiness and strength was a big mistake, but the playtime was fun. She stared up at me wide-eyed and breathing heavily.

"Thanks for the tip. You were a big help," I said as I removed the gloves and tossed them beside her outstretched body. "Enjoy your day."

CHAPTER FIVE

"HELLO, MOTHER"

It had been weeks of the same thing. Go to work, come home, talk to Clara, see Nathan, and I hated it. I preferred some doses of spontaneity, partying or malicious play, but I'd somehow gotten locked into a tedious routine.

I blamed Clara, she wanted me to lay low since we were unsure what was causing my blackouts, but I needed to breathe. There had been no thrill lately, and I was bored.

Nathan said we could go skydiving or to the gun range if I wanted to over the weekend, and I may take him up on that, but first, I needed to visit the original dragon, my mother.

She was taking her revenge on the world long before Clara and I were ever thought of. I guess, in part, my tattoo was not only a symbol of how the hunted became the hunter, but a representation of the monster that was passed down to me.

I awoke at 4 pm, and I was out the door by 4:30, dressed super cute in white shorts, a colorful shirt, and my new pink and white tennis shoes.

Just because I was going to jail didn't mean I couldn't look stylish. Luckily, the prison was only fifteen minutes away, and I arrived before visiting hours ended at 5:30.

After signing in, I sat at a table with a wobbly leg and waited for her to show. I hadn't seen her in over 6 months, and now that I considered how our last visit unfolded, maybe it was too soon.

She told me that having us was probably the stupidest decision she ever made, and I told her that it was a pity I didn't somehow kill her during childbirth. After the doctors delivered Clara and me, of course.

Either way, I didn't think she took it to heart. I know I didn't. I was here now, and there was nothing she could do about it.

I surveyed the small visitor's area and shook my head. I understood treating the prisoners poorly, but the visitors shouldn't have to suffer too; we didn't do shit.

It was fucking ridiculous how disgusting this waiting area was when they made so much money.

Then again, I guess it was their way of keeping visitors away, using it as an additional level of punishment for prisoners.

The floors were supposed to be white, but they were streaked with some brown mess that I wouldn't spend too much time wondering about.

There was a vending machine in the corner of the room, however, the contents were few, and were unappealing.

I heard the chatter increase as a few prisoners entered the room. It only took a moment to spot the woman that I was there to see. She walked over to the table and stood in front of it.

"Hi Lillian," I said, giving her a chipper wave.

"Sidney, of course. To what do I owe this honor?" Her voice was cool and disinterested.

"Nothing at all. I was bored and it made me think of you."

"Is that so?"

"Yeah, I figured who could be more bored than a woman not suitable for polite society."

She crossed her arms and smirked.

"Do you know I'm missing a very good movie for this? Make it worth my while to stay or this is goodbye."

"When did you first know you were crazy?" I asked.

That got her attention. An insane person liked nothing more than to talk about themselves.

Pulling out a chair, she took a seat and then studied me before saying, "I'm not crazy."

"Lillian, you're talking to me here. You robbed people, killed people, and knowingly left your children alone with your abusive, piece of shit brother."

"That doesn't make me crazy, that makes me misunderstood. But why do you ask?"

Everything about her was very dismissive. She barely even gave me eye contact during our exchange, instead choosing to glance appreciatively at a guard standing in the corner. I noticed him giving her the same goggly eyes. I'll bet they were fucking.

"Let's just say I want to know what makes you tick and understand how you could be so heartless."

"Not having one helps."

"True, but don't you want someone to understand why you are the way you are?"

Lillian laughed and turned her focus to the window. She was quiet for a long time, and it gave me the chance to observe her. Slouched in the chair with her arms crossed and her legs planted at least three feet apart, I wondered what she was thinking.

By looking at her, you couldn't tell she was capable of doing the things she had. Did she regret any of it? Or at some point, feel her sanity slipping away, but had no one to keep her on track?

My mother hadn't aged much and even dressed in an orange jumpsuit with her hair pulled back into a lazy ponytail and wiry pieces everywhere; she was still beautiful.

We had the same face shape and full lips. The one thing, besides life, that she gave me and I remained grateful for. She faced me again.

"If I'm going to have a heart to heart. I'd prefer to talk to Clara."

"Why, because you can scare her easily?"

"Because she isn't a bitch."

"Ouch Lillian! If I gave a fuck that could have hurt. Besides, you know Clara doesn't like to see you. The memories are still too raw for her, so today you get me," I said with an unapologetic shrug.

She bared her teeth and then exhaled. A woman at the table next to us began crying and telling the female inmate how much her kids missed her. My mom decided to chime in on their conversation.

“Don't worry, Amanda, you aren't missing anything. They grow up to be resentful and rude like this one here no matter what you do.”

“I don't doubt it Lillian, but I think mine would be better off without me.”

“That's not true!” The woman sitting with Amanda said. She began to cry harder and Amanda touched her shoulder.

Was this place a collection of unfit mothers?

Lillian butted out of their conversation now that it was becoming an emotional shit show and said, “What do you want to know, Sidney?”

"Were you always so . . ." I searched for the words. "Out of the box with your way of living?"

"I have no idea what you're talking about, you'll have to be more specific."

"Okay. Having sexual relationships with not one, but both of your brothers, robbing people, lying for sport, neglecting your children, killing the guy that landed you in here, did I miss anything?"

"Oh, those things. They all sound pretty normal to me."

"I can understand the killing part, but sleeping with your own brothers didn't phase you either?"

"Why should it? I'm a woman, they're men and we wanted each other. No need to make it complicated."

"Thankfully one of those demons is dead."

"And God rest his soul," she retorted with a smirk.

My Uncle Trevor had a brother named Damien that my mom was equally...umm... affectionate with. However, Damien was killed when Clara and I were babies, a bullet to the head from what I hear.

The only heartbreaking part was that his sadistic brother Trevor, and maybe Lillian, weren't destroyed with him.

"You're sick, Lillian."

"Pot meet kettle!" she snapped back.

"Fair enough. Your brother isn't my dad, is he?"

"Do you look like him?!"

She responded as if the question was stupid. In her defense, it probably was. Some of these features definitely came from someone outside of our family tree, but I had to ask.

"Back to the abuse. You didn't care that he was raping your daughters?"

She eyed me.

"Not this again. Didn't I apologize to you for that?"

"You do know an apology doesn't fix it, right?"

"So what would you have me do?" She motioned around the building. "I'm already in jail, sweetie."

"Maybe they could find you a darker cell?"

She laughed, and I smiled at her. We did this dance every visit. Maybe I wanted answers and hadn't been able to accept that she didn't have them. Or maybe there was something deeper.

Leaning back in her chair, she examined me for what had to be the third time that day.

"Oh, I get it now. You think you're turning into me. That's what this is all about."

That hurt. I was surprised at how the sudden truth offended me. I didn't mind being vindictive, heartless, or even psychotic. It was my trademark, and I liked who I was.

The insanity made my personality spicy. But now it was ruined because she compared me to her!

We watched each other in silence for a long beat, both unapologetic in our deranged zones of normal.

"No nothing like you. Maybe, I'm worse."

"Maybe," she agreed. "The child is ten times the parent."

Lillian stood.

"Well, this has been fun, but I have better things to do."

"I agree," I replied, standing.

I thought she would walk away, but she remained in place.

"You've grown to be a beautiful girl Sidney, and I'm certain you can have a great life, but after being in this place over ten years, let me offer you some motherly advice."

"Because you love me?" I asked with a disingenuous smile.

"Not really, and before you comment, I already know the feeling is mutual, but you are my daughter, and I figure that should count for something."

"What's the advice? Don't be as twisted as you?"

She laughed, "Not at all dear," and then she sobered. "Don't get caught."

I elected not to go straight home. Going to the park first to do some reading seemed like a better plan, especially since I was in a wonderful mood and didn't have to work tonight. I called Nathan on the bus ride to the park.

"How'd your visit with your mom go?"

"It was nice. I can't complain."

"Was she happy to see you?"

"I'm not sure if Lillian is ever happy."

"Wow. That must suck I can't imagine only knowing my mom through prison."

That was because he didn't have to imagine it. He had an amazing, caring, and generous mother that loved him and spent a lot of time telling him so.

I actually never had second thoughts about the relationship that Lillian and I had until I met Nathan's mother.

Would being raised by someone like her from birth have made a difference in who I was today? Probably, but we would never know.

"What are you doing right now?" I asked.

"Now, I am in the inventory room staring at 50 boxes that I have to put up by tomorrow."

"Sucks to be you."

"It does. I wish I could blow off work and come see you."

"No need. Absence makes the heart grow fonder and we will see each other this weekend, remember?"

"If I wasn't so sure you liked me, I'd think you were brushing me off."

Probably because I was. No offense to him, but I wanted my alone time.

"I'm sorry, I simply want to sit at my favorite bench and read."

I pressed the alert so the bus driver could know I wanted to get off at the next stop.

"I know how you are and I love you anyway."

"You're the best, Nathan."

"So you tell me," he said.

We ended the call and I exited the bus. I could see that my favorite bench was free. Could this day get any better? I almost ran to it but something horrible stopped me in my tracks.

Mrs. Larks was standing near it with Bella, and that mutt was shitting near my bench! My fucking bench!

Breathe Sidney. I remind myself as the voices of Clara and Lillian also sprang into my mind.

"Trouble doesn't get started on its own," Clara had said.

"Don't get caught," Lillian had warned me.

They were right. I had to be smart and collect my composure. Going into war mode on Mrs. Larks was messy and unnecessary.

I squeezed my fist tight, causing my nails to dig deep into my palm. The pain helped some of the irritation subside and my vision focused. I calmly walked the rest of the way to the bench.

"Excuse me," I said in the most polite voice I could manage.

Hearing myself speak aloud, I was impressed. There was no way she would be able to tell that I was holding back from scrubbing her face on the concrete.

“Yeah, what do you want?" Mrs. Larks said in a gruff tone. Her voice was raspy and a little deep. She must have been a smoker. I glanced at the dog. She was still squatting and relieving herself.

“Are you going to pick that up?”

Her lips tightened, and her jaw clenched. Now that I

was seeing her up close. I placed her to be in her late 50's to early 60's.

"What's it to you? Are you the park police?" she said with a cough.

Yup, definitely a smoker. Ms. Darcy used to smoke. I would never forget that annoying, wheezing, wet sound. So glad I ended her. Continuing to remain calm, I answered her rudely asked question.

"No. I'm not. I'm simply a concerned citizen. It's inconsiderate not to clean up after your dog. I've stepped in it at least four times now and I'd appreciate you not making it a fifth."

"You don't know that it was my dog," she retorted.

My left hand felt damp. I must have drawn blood.

"Yes. I. Do."

I was spacing my words. Not a good sign. She cackled as if I had said something extremely funny. The dog finished up its business and came to stand beside her. It looked up at me and tilted its head.

"So you're a poop detective, now? Get out of my face I don't owe you anything."

"You're not going to clean it up?" I asked, my voice rising slightly.

"No, why should I? She's a dog and this is nature. Nature will take care of it."

I stepped a little closer to her.

"Today, *you* will take care of it," I said, pointing a finger at her pudgy face.

"Who's going to make me?"

My lips curved upward, and I took a step back. She was pleased and obviously full of herself. I truly hoped she had room for a little more.

I bent down, and with my right hand, I picked up the dog poop.

The look on her face could have made a viral meme on the internet in seconds. I watched her expression shift from speechless to disbelief to horror. The horror I liked. It looked good on her, but not better than the dog shit I smashed into her face.

She screamed and started wiping frantically at her mouth. Several people stopped to see what was going on.

"Nothing to see here!" I yelled. "She's my sick grandmother and thought she saw a ghost."

Everyone that stopped resumed minding their business and gave me sympathetic looks and pitying smiles.

One guy even yelled from across the grass, "You're a good granddaughter!"

I looked back at the woman, she was in shock, visibly shaking. Her dog had even taken a few steps back from her. Apparently, Bella didn't like the new scent her owner was wearing.

"You are a cruel woman. I am going to have you arrested."

She started angrily rummaging through her purse; for her cellphone I assumed. I took that as my cue to exit.

Before I did, I bent down to pet the dog, using the hand that still had a slight trace of feces. She was a good dog. Happy to get any affection and her nice sleek fur served as the perfect rag.

"Get away from my dog!" Mrs. Larks yelled, pulling the leash.

I had no idea why she was so mad. It was the dog's shit, after all. I was simply helping nature take care of itself.

CHAPTER SIX

"THAT'S A HORRIBLE THING TO SAY."

My eyes popped open, and were immediately assaulted by the bright glow of the sun beaming through the window. I closed my eyes and turned my head. When I opened them again, I noticed Clara's best friend Barbara sitting in a chair staring at me. The girl was creepy.

I glanced at the clock on the bookshelf. It was 3:45 pm. I didn't remember coming home from the park or putting my pajamas on, but here I was at home and clothed in sleepwear. I must have had another blackout. Ugh, this sucked!

I covered my face and said, "What do you want, Barbara?"

"Just to see how you're doing?"

"Well, you've seen me. I'm in one piece. Thanks for stopping by."

I sat up, and my head hurt. Should have remained flat.

"Are you okay, Sidney?" Barbara asked.

"I'm fine Barbara. Why aren't you somewhere bothering Clara?"

She ignored my question.

"Clara is worried about you. Between the blackouts and your erratic behavior. I told her I would try to talk to you."

I was going to strangle Clara.

“I really appreciate the concern, but I'm fine."

I took a second to close my eyes. Then meditated on pushing the pain thumping behind them back to hell where it must have come from... but had no luck.

"Are you sure, Sidney? You can talk to me."

I turned towards her then. I needed to be loud and clear about her position in my life.

"Barbara. I tolerate your invasive questioning because you are Clara's friend, but I don’t need a psychiatrist. If I did, I would choose someone that already has a degree."

Barbara wasn’t phased by my snappy attitude. I assumed she must be used to it by now.

“Not officially having a degree doesn’t mean I can’t help, Sidney. If you don’t deal with the trauma from your childhood, it won't vanish. It will only release itself in another way."

"Haven't you already talked to Clara about our childhood?"

"Yes, but I want to hear from you."

“Copy your notes from her version, put my name at the top and voilà session complete,” I said, snapping my fingers.

Barbara exhaled quietly.

“Alright Sidney, I get it. You aren’t ready to talk. If you ever change your mind I’m here, okay?"

My response was to walk into the kitchen and let Barbara show herself out. I heard soft music coming from Clara’s room. Typical.

She was hiding, too afraid to come out and face me after throwing me to the wolves, or in Barbara's case, a pup, who should get a few years under her belt before trying her hand at me.

Barbara left the apartment without another word, and I stood in front of an overflowing trash can.

Usually, Clara takes it out before school, but for the past

few days, she'd forgotten. I went to the bathroom to wash up and then took it out.

On my way back up to my apartment, I noticed Shelly sitting on a stair.

Her hands were folded in her lap, and she looked worried, she also appeared sick and frail, but that was nothing new, considering who she was shacking up with.

I had nothing against the girl. I truly disliked her boyfriend, but I was going to mind my own business.

I had just made it past her when she said, "Tell Clara thank you."

"For?"

"She gave me something very helpful, that's all."

Her answer was vague, and I didn't care enough to question her further. Between selling me out to Barbara and assisting Shelly with whatever it was, Clara had been a very busy girl.

"I'll tell her," I said and walked away.

When I entered our apartment, Clara had emerged. She was in the kitchen, doing what came naturally, studying. A cup of juice and a turkey sandwich sat on the table.

The sandwich was cut in half so that it formed two triangles. It was the way Grandma Nancy always did for us. Somehow sandwiches tasted better when she added her special touch.

Clara held on to a lot of things from our childhood. I guess it gave her comfort.

"Hi Sidney!" she said, smiling.

"Don't even try it. Seriously, Barbara?!"

"I know, I know, but I'm running out of options. I think you need to speak to someone and I feel like you aren't listening to me anymore."

"You're right. When your answer is always to turn the other cheek, I stop listening."

She looked down at the sandwich and then back up at me. It was her way of offering me half. I picked it up and sat down.

“Have you been working on remaining calm?” Clara asks.

I don’t know why she is pretending to be clueless. From the look in her eyes, she knows something. Clara has a knack for figuring out things I have done and I don’t know how.

As uneventful as her life may be, I still don’t know what goes on in it unless she tells me. I took a bite of the sandwich.

"Mmhmm," I said, nodding my head and chewing.

"You’re lying, I know about the park incident.”

Damn it! Clara strikes again.

“How?!" I asked over a mouth full of food.

"I have my ways, but Sidney, dog poop? Really?"

“Clara, she had it coming."

“Regardless, not only did you draw attention to yourself, you likely can’t go back to that park for a while.”

I knew she was right. I had considered that myself. Nevertheless, I would do it again in a heartbeat. I didn’t believe in regrets. They were a tricky and manipulative emotion that easily got out of hand.

Regretting turned into sadness and sadness turned into depression. My emotional load was already maxed out dealing with Clara and her feelings.

I took another bite of my sandwich. It was delicious. Clara definitely made better food than me. It was why she was in charge of cooking. I could barely boil water.

“I won’t be getting into any more trouble."

"You're lying, again. But you know what? If you want to punish the world, go to jail and end up like mom, that's your business.”

"Finally! You see things my way."

Clara rolled her eyes and closed her book. I think she was learning about medical terminology this week.

"Speaking of minding your own business, Clara, Shelly told me to tell you thanks. What's that all about?"

Clara shrugged.

"I gave her a pamphlet on abuse that included a list of shelters so that she could get help."

"Why? She isn't going to use it," I said.

"You don't know that."

"And neither do you."

"Sidney, being abused by someone is not easy to escape."

"Yes, it is. Wait until he falls asleep and slit his throat."

"Everyone isn't like you. Maybe she's afraid of him."

"That explains why she is a victim," I responded, annoyed.

"That's a horrible thing to say!"

"That's a true thing to say. Instead of being the victim, she should turn the tables and vict-him."

"Vict-him?"

"Evict him from his fucking body."

"That's my sister, ladies and gentleman," she announced. "Ready to destroy anyone that crosses her."

"Or you and Grandma," I added.

"You better be glad I love you and you make me laugh or else I'd go and live with Barbara."

"I'd like to see that. Barbara would put you out on your ass the first time you woke up screaming. By the way, does Barbara have any friends besides you?"

"A few, why?"

"I was wondering why she doesn't hang around them more. Wait let me guess, you're the most interesting?"

"Knock her all you want Sidney, but we have fun

together. And look who's talking. Besides Nathan you don't deal with anyone else."

"I hang out with Cassie and as far as Nathan goes he's sweet, fun and doesn't ask me a lot of questions."

"And that makes you comfortable, right?"

"I don't need Nathan to make me comfortable, I'm always comfortable."

"My point is, Barbara makes me comfortable. She's easy to talk to and if I don't want to talk that's fine too. She's been a good friend and I'm grateful for her."

"Alright, fine I get it! Killing Barbara is off limits."

"That's not exactly the point I was making, but I'd appreciate it if you didn't."

I could honor that request. It's not like Clara had much and Barbara did seem to make her happy. We finished our food while chatting about nothing too deep.

Afterward, we played a game of chess, called to check on Grandma and then Clara helped me pick out a shirt to pair with my sexy jeans for work.

Things were slow at the bar tonight. I spent a whole hour playing on social media without disruption. I loved how everyone always wanted to be seen and heard online.

The more I learned about people's behaviors, the easier they became to manipulate and then if necessary, eliminate.

"Do you think you can handle the bar for about twenty minutes?" Cassie asked.

I scanned the bar. There were only ten people sitting around at various tables.

"Sure. It's pretty dead in here."

"You're right, make it forty-five minutes instead. I'm going to go on a smoke break and flirt with the guard at the club next door. Who knows, maybe I will find us a fun party to go to."

I gave her a thumbs up and went back to scrolling through my phone. A few minutes went by and still no one. I decided to respond to Nathan's text he'd sent twenty minutes ago.

As soon as I pressed send, I heard a deep voice in front of me say, "If you weren't on your phone maybe you could do a better job of taking orders."

I glanced up. A large man with short spiky hair and bloodshot eyes had sat down. I overlooked the audacious remark and approached the counter.

"How may I help you?"

"Give me a glass of Krupnik."

"Coming right up."

I checked the lower cabinet where Grid normally kept the polish liquor and found nothing.

Krupnik wasn't a popular drink at the bar, but Grid liked to keep it in stock for the few customers that enjoyed some familiarity of home.

I checked the next cabinet and found the bottle, but it was empty. Krupnik was something that Grid special ordered himself, and it looked like he forgot to do so.

I picked up the bottle and returned to the guy.

"Sorry, we're out," I said, holding it up.

"What the fuck do you mean?"

I repeated my previous statement. He already appeared wasted. He probably shouldn't have been drinking anymore, anyway.

He slammed an angry fist down on the counter. A couple sitting at a table in the back jumped. I slid my hand down by the lemons and locked my fingers around the slicing knife.

"Now, you listen to me, little girl. When Grid is here he

always takes care of me, but for some reason I guess he decided to let the children handle grown folk's business. Why don't you march your cute little ass in the back and find me some more."

Murder is not mandatory. Murder is not mandatory.

My mind was populating scenarios of retaliation before I could stop it. It was simply my knee-jerk reaction to things.

I took a deep breath, still clenching the knife, and heard Clara's voice, scared and alone, warning me not to overreact.

I let go of the knife and smiled.

"Let me see what I can do."

I grabbed the empty glass bottle and went to the back-room. I searched around for a new bottle in case Grid had some back here, but as expected, found nothing.

I considered returning and restating, yet again, that we were out, and daring him to get out of hand. However, that would be poking the bear for no reason.

The guy was already drunk or at least tipsy. I might be able to give him something close, and he wouldn't even notice the difference.

I recalled that Krupnik was a yellow drink with spiced vodka and honey. That basically meant it was sweet and spicy. I grabbed a bottle of vodka from the top shelf and poured it in, filling the bottle up a quarter of the way.

Now for something spicy and sweet. I grabbed some black pepper and honey, adding both ingredients to the bottle in unequal amounts. I figured adding more honey than black pepper would be effective enough.

I shook the bottle up and black specs from the pepper were visibly swirling around. I shrugged; it was dim in the bar, he wasn't likely to notice.

Now, all I needed was to match the color. I looked

around for something that would give the drink its sunny appearance. Nothing stood out, but that's when I realized that I was looking outward when I should've been looking inward.

I put the bottle down and grabbed a plastic cup that I proceeded to pee into. Emptying my bladder, I considered maybe I really did have a problem.

Should I talk to Barbara? She could give me some insight.

Then almost immediately, I disregarded the whole idea. All I was doing was serving a specialty drink to a man that I could have easily followed out behind the bar and stabbed in the chest. That showed I had self-control.

I finished up and added the last ingredient to the bottle. It didn't look perfect, but it should suffice. I walked back out and held up the bottle.

"You're in luck! There was a little bit left back there."

"Good girl," he said. "Give me two shots."

I prepared the requested amount and placed them in front of him. He downed both shots quickly, then smacked his lips.

Fucking pig.

"That's what I'm talking about."

He paused as if to think and said, "It tastes less spicy than I'm used to, but I'll take it. Give me another round, sweet cheeks."

Inside I cringed at the pet name, but outside I gave him my most genuine smile and placed the bottle on the counter in front of him.

"You can have the rest of the bottle, sir. It's on the house."

CHAPTER SEVEN

"HE HOWLED IN PAIN."

I dashed to the left and then to the right. I could see the red lasers moving all around me, but they couldn't find me. I was too crafty. I was hunched down in a corner with my back against a tall structure in a tiny area behind a short wall.

Nathan was visible from where I squat. He was peeking around a corner, likely looking for me and about to suffer for his ignorance. I aimed at his chest and pulled the trigger.

"You're dead," I said with a chilling smile.

"Damn, you always get me."

I stood, revealing my hiding spot.

"What can I say? You're an easy target."

He pulled me in for a kiss, but I broke it off before it got too intense. I forgot to remove my razor blade today. He looked at me awkwardly, or at least I assumed he did, it was pretty dark in here.

"Everything cool, Sidney?"

"Yeah. Sad that the game is over, that's all."

"I think you enjoy this game a little too much. You want to play another round?"

I covered my mouth, faking a yawn, and discreetly pushed the small, covered metal piece out with my tongue and slid it into my back jeans pocket.

"No. I guess that was enough of an adrenaline rush for today. Let's go find something else to do."

"Whatever you say my little assassin."

This time I kissed him. It was my way of saying thank you. Nathan was the type of man love stories were written about. I had no idea how I got so lucky... karma I guess. He grabbed my hand, and we exited the game area.

Once outside the pretend war zone, we removed all of our gear and checked the scores. As usual, mine topped his.

I remember when we first began coming to this mall to play laser tag. I always thought he was letting me win.

As time moved on, I realized he was simply that weak, and my practice at the gun range was benefiting me more than I knew.

We stopped by a shopping booth located directly outside of the laser tag entrance so that Nathan could get me a stuffed animal, his idea, not mine.

I wasn't sure if Nathan thought that he had to buy things to keep me. True, I didn't love him and probably never would, but I liked him plenty.

"You want the big fluffy dog?" he asked.

I thought about Bella and the poop that ruined my shoes and frowned.

"You don't have to get me anything. You always bring me things from your job, like the voice recorder and wireless EarPods. I don't need anything else."

He waved off my protest and pointed to something small and shiny inside the clear display shelf.

"What about that?"

It was a badge that read 'Laser Tag Star'.

"I guess that's okay."

He purchased it from the guy and pinned it to my shirt.

"Perfect fit," he said, looking into my eyes. "You ready to go?"

His eyes were warm and sincere. It made me wonder if anyone could truly be that kind and not have a hidden agenda.

Staring at him, with his love for me apparent in his gaze, I could only think one thing; I hoped no one murdered him. Hell, I hope I didn't murder him. Terrible things always happen to the best people.

"Sure," I said, taking his hand.

Since we were in the mall, I decided to take advantage and do some much-needed shopping. I collected three new pairs of heels.

Black, gold, and a red pair I had been eyeing for over a month. In addition to the shoes, I got a few more skirts and halter tops.

I modeled them for Nathan, and the naughty thoughts being broadcasted through his stare were welcomed. If he thought it looked hot, so would the inebriated clientele at the bar.

We wrapped it up with me buying some jeans and more bunny slippers for Clara and me to share. She would be so excited when she saw them.

Exiting the mall through the food court, a man sitting with three other guys called out to Nathan.

I mentally sighed; it was his stupid work buddies. I couldn't stand them, especially the one that had called out to him. His name was Mitch, and he was a waste of space. I spat in his drink every time I served him at the bar.

My dislike for Mitch began one night when Nathan's entire team showed up at the bar celebrating their month of record-breaking sales.

I remember approaching the table to greet Nathan when I overheard Mitch telling him that he could have at least picked a girl that wouldn't make him wait for sex.

Immediately my anger flared. Who the fuck did that

limp dick bastard think he was to be giving others advice? He was in his late 40's, fat, sloppy, and had already been divorced three times!

When I asked Nathan about it later that night, he said Mitch had inquired about my bedroom skills, and he responded that we were taking it slow.

The part I walked in on was Mitch's rude response to that idea. Watching Mitch now, as Nathan guided us closer to the table to say hello, I was annoyed that we weren't at the bar right now so that I could add my special ingredient.

"Hey, Nathan, what brings you to the mall?" Mitch asked.

The other guys lifted their hands in greeting, but I guess Mitch would be doing most of the talking.

"Just finished up a game of laser tag and some shopping." Then, placing the attention on me, he added, "Everyone you remember, Sidney?"

All four guys gave another round of nods. Two of them stared at me a little too long, but only Mitch got under my skin. He licked his lips and gave me a quick once over.

"Hey Sidney, you working the bar tonight?" Mitch asked.

"Nope," was my only response.

He directed the conversation back to Nathan.

"We were sitting here hoping some hot girls would be roaming around, but it's been pretty boring." He narrowed his eyes, "Maybe we should have been playing around in the dark like the two of you."

The statement was slathered in sexual innuendo. Mitch laughed at his simple-minded comment, and the other spineless losers chimed in.

That's it, I was about to burst his bubble. I unpinned the button Nathan had just purchased for me from my shirt and held it in my hand. I readjusted the needle so that it stuck straight out. I don't think anyone saw me.

"I don't know what you're implying Mitch. We only played laser tag, and as always my baby got the highest score."

He lifted my hand and kissed it. Such a gentleman.

"I know you two like to keep it clean, I was just fucking around with you. Are you going to be at work tomorrow?"

"Yeah, I got the morning shift so I'll be there bright and early."

"Guess I'll see you on your way out. I don't come in until three."

We'll see about that. I thought to myself.

They talked for another few minutes about nothing of importance before Nathan said goodbye. As we were leaving, I pretended to trip over one of the chairs and fell onto Mitch's lap, stabbing him in the leg with the pin.

He howled in pain, and I landed on the floor beside his chair.

Nathan immediately assisted me to my feet.

"You okay, Sidney?"

His hands were frantically checking me for scrapes and bruises.

"I'm fine," I responded, feigning confusion. "I must have tripped."

Nathan looks at Mitch. The man was pulling at the 'Laser Tag Star' badge.

"Damn, man, are you alright?" Nathan asked the big cry baby.

"Shit, shit, shit!" Mitch shouts.

The pin was still lodged into the area slightly above his knee. He was wearing shorts, and I could see a trickle of blood oozing out. The sight of it made me giggle. I covered my mouth and pretended to be shocked.

"Oh, Mitch, I'm so sorry. I guess the pin wasn't completely closed."

"Yeah, it looks like you got me good there. But I'm okay," he grunted, his country accent really taking over. He finally freed the pin from its unfortunate prison and blinked a few times. Beads of sweat poured off of his forehead down to his meaty cheeks.

Fat ass.

He picked up a napkin from the table and dabbed at the blood on his leg.

"Are you okay?" he asked me.

His question was surprising. I assumed he would be more self-centered given what I knew about him. See how kind people can be when there is pain involved?

"I'm great, Mitch. Thanks for asking." My choice of words may have been a bit too lively, but no one commented.

Nathan gave Mitch one last look of pity and placed an arm around my shoulder.

"Well, we are going to get out of here. Let me know if you need to call in or be a little late tomorrow."

"It's no big deal," Mitch said through a tight chuckle. "I've been through worse."

Now that we had confirmed that Mitch was going to live to see another day, we collected my bags and headed for the mall exit. Nathan commented how weird it was that the pin came undone and stabbed poor Mitch.

"That is weird, but life is like that sometimes," I replied.

It was close to 7 pm, and I'd had such a wonderful day. At the moment I was in a fantastic mood. Glancing up at Nathan, I asked, "Are you in the mood for ice cream?"

Nathan dropped me off in front of my apartment building. He'd forgotten to pick up something for his mom at the pharmacy, so I told him there was no need to help me get inside with my bags.

Besides, I was still floating on cloud nine. Nothing could ruin this day.

Why, oh why, was I so wrong?

The moment I made it to the staircase, I heard the pitiful, agitating voice of Marcus belittling Shelly.

"Excuses, excuses. That's all you fucking give me!"

Why didn't someone put a bullet in this man already? His destructive nature was ruining my perfect day.

"I'm sorry Marcus," Shelly pleaded. "I really am. Please don't be mad. I haven't been feeling well."

"More excuses. You're good for nothing, you know that? I should have left your dumb, useless ass on the street where I found you."

I heard Shelly's sobs kick up a notch. They got louder and vibrated through me as I climbed the stairs getting closer to my apartment.

"Oh did that hurt your feelings?" Marcus stated in a mocking tone. "Get over it! Why weren't you out working today? Our bills are going to be late because of you. You're such a fucking waste."

"I told you I wasn't feeling well and I think my period is coming on."

"So what? Your mouth works doesn't it?"

Damn, even I had to admit that was cold. I climbed the last flight of stairs that would deliver me face to face with the predator and his prey.

There was a sudden shriek of pain and Shelly shouting for him to let her go. I guess Marcus had decided to incorporate his hands into the disagreement.

I rounded the corner just as he was dragging her back into their apartment. He shoved her inside, and she fell on the floor, gripping her stomach.

"Stop playing around and get ready to make me some money!"

Poor girl. She should sharpen her knives more often.

Marcus grabbed the knob, but right before closing it, he said, "Now stay in there until I get back." He slammed it shut and started walking in my direction. I thought nothing of it because it led to the stairs.

"Hey, little Miss Nosy," he said, stopping in front of me.

I stood still and glanced around. There was no way he could be speaking to me. However, no one else was in the hallway. I looked up at him. He wasn't that tall or intimidating in my opinion, but he was an asshole with quite the chip on his shoulder.

"You and your sister need to mind your own fucking business. Shelly doesn't need your help, your pamphlets, or your pity. I run my place however the hell I want to."

I simply stared at him. Normally I would be sizing him up, but honestly, I was caught off guard. It was both offensive and astonishing that he thought I was another version of Shelly.

A woman that would take his threats, cowering in fear and begging for his forgiveness.

His assumption was inaccurate, and his life was losing value with every word he spoke.

He continued, oblivious to the disastrous door he had just opened.

"If I catch either of you meddling in my personal affairs again, you'll be sorry."

With that, he walked past me towards the stairs bumping my shoulder so hard, a bag slipped from my hand, and I had to grab onto the banister to keep from falling.

I was seething on the inside. Voices of fury awakened and wanted blood . . . Marcus's blood, and I would feed them. It was unfortunate too, because I was doing so good.

Too bad Marcus had just upgraded himself from my shit list to my hit list.

CHAPTER EIGHT

"YOU'RE GOING TO KILL HIM AREN'T YOU?"

"He won't get away with this."

My tone perfectly conveyed my mood. Calm, certain, and honestly a little bored.

The planning of retaliation was becoming less exciting. I needed to witness the pain and horrified shock in my victims to give me the satisfied feeling I sought nowadays.

I wasn't sure what I wanted to do to Marcus, but his detestable, arrogant behavior necessitated some creative thinking.

"Sidney, it was merely a threat. An empty threat. He isn't going to hurt me or you."

I looked at Clara as if she came from another planet.

"Are we talking about the same guy? The guy that beats Shelly's ass for recreation?" I asked.

Her face scrunched up. She clearly hadn't thought that part of her argument through.

"Alright, yes, he could be dangerous. But that's the point, he *could* be. We will simply do what he says and mind our own business and everyone is happy."

I raised my hand.

"I won't be happy."

"Sidney!"

"What, I won't. He's a bully and you know how I feel about bullies."

She sat down on the couch.

"You're going to kill him aren't you?"

"Haven't decided yet. Sometimes there are things worse than death. I think Marcus deserves those other things."

Clara straightened in her chair and fixed her eyes on the wall behind me. We were at the kitchen table and I was eating some leftover lasagna she'd made, while she was fighting an inward battle over the right thing to do. I cleared half of the food on my plate before Clara spoke again.

"I don't think it's worth it."

She was still trying to find an out for Marcus. Fuck that, he had dug himself in way too deep.

"When he threatened us, he basically offed himself. I merely want to assist with the disposal."

"No!" she said standing and pointing a finger at me. "You are going to keep taking the high road. You cannot even the score with the world no matter . . ."

I zoned out and lifted my hand to stare at my nails. Currently, they were cotton candy pink. It was time for a change.

A beautiful yellow would be nice, or maybe a blood red. I smiled to myself. Yes, blood red. That would go perfectly with my red skirt and black shirt. I even had various shades of red lipstick to jazz it up even more.

"Are you listening to me, Sidney?" Clara said, cutting into my thoughts.

"How could I not? You're practically in my head. Stressing me nonstop about my actions towards people that don't deserve to live."

Clara slowly shook her head and laughed to herself.

"There is no winning with you is there?"

"I'll give you one guess."

She looked at me, trying desperately to make me waiver, by using her eyes and sheer will. It didn't work. I'm not sure why she thought it would. I wasn't budging, but even though she knew this, she always tried.

Being the more thoughtful, civil version of me, it was her duty to keep the peace. I understood her position, but I had my own.

"Fine!" she said, finally giving up. "Meet me halfway and promise not to kill him."

"I will not kill him."

I answered her too fast and she stared at me, waiting for me to say something along the lines of, just kidding.

However, I didn't. Full transparency I know I lie a lot, but I wasn't lying when I said I didn't want to kill Marcus. I wanted to do something to him that he would have to live with for the rest of his life and be tortured by it.

Clara decided to sit down again and change the subject. Nowadays, my sweet sister was getting better at knowing when fighting me on a matter was pointless.

She pointed at the new pink bunny slippers I got at the mall. They were over by the couch, looking fluffy and inviting.

"Those for us?"

"More so you. Do you like them?"

"Of course. The others have a huge hole in them. My feet were getting drafty."

"Why didn't you grab some new ones?"

"You know how sentimental I can be."

I nodded. Sentimental was an understatement. She was often too prone to the nauseating emotions of nostalgia and sadness. Which is why I hated sharing bad news with her.

"Want to play a game of chess?" Clara asked with a smile.

"Sure. I have a couple of hours before work."

"No cheating," she said, pointedly.

"No promises."

Clara put her hands on her hips and gave me a stern look over her glasses. It reminded me of grandma and I laughed a little. My sister was way too young to be acting so old.

"Sidney, I literally let you get away with murder, but cheating during chess is where I draw the line."

I lifted my hands in surrender.

"Fine, whatever you say older half."

"So glad you could see it my way," Clara responded, grabbing the game.

I wrecked my brain during my entire shift trying to figure out the perfect way to give Marcus a dose of his own cold, cruel medicine. But every scenario I came up with only ended with him dead.

From tying him up, and then inserting syringe-filled household cleaning products into his veins, to using a funnel and pouring ground-up glass down his throat, to a good old fashion gunshot to the head. He wouldn't survive any of them.

Damn it. Was I losing my touch?

I was only 20 years old. My best years of revenge had to be ahead of me, not behind. I had to be smart about it and not let my impulses lead. I certainly didn't want to end up in prison bunking with Lillian.

I'd have to kill that bitch or she'd kill me and poor Clara would simply end up caught in the crossfire.

I arrived home at my usual time, a little after midnight, and found Shelly sitting on the stairs.

I rarely ran into her this late; Marcus must not have

been home. She always sat on the stairs when he wasn't there.

It was an odd thing, but their whole dynamic was odd to me. I knew she could go inside when she wanted to, I'd seen her do it.

However, in this case, maybe being outside was better than being in.

Her head was down, and I could hear light sniffling. She must have been crying. I almost walked past her, but then thought better of it. Not because I cared, but because Marcus told me not to speak to her again. Defying him felt right.

"Are you okay?"

Her head jerked up, and she looked startled. Maybe she didn't hear me approaching. She was definitely crying or at least she had been. Her eyes were red and puffy. Shelly quickly wiped them.

"I . . . uhh . . . I'm okay."

My silence remained intact as I watched her.

"No, I'm not!" she suddenly said, followed by more crying.

"*Be nice Sidney,*" I could hear Clara saying. That damn sister of mine had worked her way into my head with her constant 'Kumbaya' speeches.

I took a deep breath, released it, and sat next to Shelly.

Dammit, Clara, you owe me.

"What's wrong?" I asked, desperately trying to drum up some interest and concern.

"I'm pregnant."

Okay, that might do it. I don't know what I expected her to say, but it wasn't that.

"Is it his?" I asked.

I'm sure she knew why I asked. Marcus forced her into

prostitution, and there was certainly a possibility that that baby could have belonged to someone else.

She nodded. Her voice was so shaky and small when she said, "I always have the men use protection, and for the last few months, I haven't had sex with anyone, except Marcus." She laughed to herself, but it was obvious she didn't think anything was funny. "I've been convincing the guys to let me give them oral or hand jobs instead."

I was completely grossed out by her confession. I couldn't settle myself to want one man touching me in that way.

Here it was she was letting things happen with total strangers, and society considered people like me crazy. Go figure.

"What are you going to do?"

"I want to keep it."

An odd feeling washed over me. One that was unfamiliar. I suddenly wanted Shelly to be okay, to make it through this.

What the hell!?

An outpour of memories from my own childhood, of being sexually abused by my uncle, hit, yelled at, and in constant fear flashed at lightning speed through my mind. No child should ever have to live through something like that.

"You sure you want to keep it?" I asked.

She shrugged.

"Yes. But I have nowhere to go."

"I thought Clara gave you a brochure with local shelters?"

"She did and I memorized the address and phone numbers before Marcus ripped it up. But how would I get there? I have no money. Marcus certainly wouldn't give it to me."

"You don't have any family you could call?"

I was surprising myself with these questions. It wasn't like me to get into other people's messes.

"I have an aunt in Texas that I could live with, but she wouldn't have any extra money to send for me."

"I think you should go to your aunt," I said.

A nice little plan of how to repay Marcus was forming in my head.

"I just told you I don't have any money."

"Don't worry about the money, I'll give it to you."

Her eyes widened.

"You'd give me the money?"

Ugh, she was starting to annoy me, again. Why didn't she understand this wasn't about her? It was about her baby. The innocent child that deserved so much better and me evening the score with a man who had met his match.

"Yeah, I'll give you the money."

Momentarily she appeared happy. The possibility of being away from Marcus and his abuse made her eyes dance with joy and relief. Nonetheless, as quickly as the joy came, it seemed to vanish.

Shelly shook her head frantically.

"Marcus will come looking for me. He will be so angry if he finds me."

"Does he know about your aunt?"

"No, but—"

"Then you have no problems," I said. "Besides, I'm going to slow Marcus down for you."

Her brows knitted together in confusion.

"What do you mean?"

"Don't worry about it. Do you want this chance to leave or not?"

"I do . . . I just . . ."

Damn this girl and her hesitance. This level of fear

created by another human being was new territory for me and fucking ridiculous.

Grow a pair. End this madness. She was still saying something. Talking herself out of her one chance for escape, I assumed. I cut in, again.

"You know Shelly, if I weren't mistaken I would think you don't mind Marcus beating your ass every day."

Her mouth fell open, and I could see her hurt at my remark. Good. She needed to be shocked into waking the fuck up. Obviously, she wasn't a mean girl, merely a misguided one.

I continued, "Marcus is a nobody, not some secret agent. I'm going to give you enough money to go to your aunt. Take the opportunity and save your own life and the life of your child before he kills you both."

She was silent for a long time then said, "But I'm scared of him."

"I'll bet your baby will be, too."

Tears filled her eyes again, but this time it seemed to be tears of relief.

"How will I ever repay you?"

I smiled at her.

"I'm going to need a key to your place.

I called off work the following night to meet up with Shelly. She told me that Marcus wouldn't return until close to 1 am. Which was perfect for my idea. She came over to my apartment at 10 o'clock. Clara was asleep, which meant I could handle everything I needed to without the guilt.

When Shelly gave me the key to her place, the one thing I had requested from her, I gave her a thick envelope of cash in exchange. I could tell by the expression on her face that she was shocked I had given her so much money.

"How much is this?" she asked in a whisper.

"$2,000," I responded, studying the key.

Shelly made a sound that fell between a laugh and a sob. It was really no big deal; I had over 50K saved up. It wasn't hard for me to save since I barely spent any money.

Nathan usually paid for everything, and even before him, I always found ways to cushion my account.

Not to mention, I was still pocketing money from the bar. Grid was a nice guy, and I respected him, but he offered no 401K, so I had to wing it.

"Thank you so much, Sidney."

She tried to hug me, but I stopped her. We were not friends.

"I have given you enough money to make a fresh start with your baby. Don't go looking for a new guy to victimize you."

She lowered her arms.

"I understand. Will you tell Clara I said goodbye?"

"I will."

When her hand touched the knob, I called out to her. After she faced me I said "By the way, get a gun. You might be afraid of Marcus, but a bullet isn't."

She nodded and left, pulling the door closed quietly behind her. She had an Uber waiting downstairs to take her to the airport. I knew one thing, I better not ever see her around here again, or Marcus would be the last person she would have to worry about.

I changed my clothes and dressed in all black. I planned to wear black gloves and a black full-face mask as well, but for now, I set them aside.

I walked through my apartment collecting a few specific things I would need, such as handcuffs, a small roll of duct tape, the gun I hid underneath my clothes, and the voice changer gifted to me by Nathan.

I was so excited that I was finally going to get to use it! I locked the straps behind my ears and pulled the square piece over my mouth. Then I pulled on the face mask.

I wanted to test it to be sure that it would work perfectly and I could be heard easily. I was so delighted when it did that I performed a quick dance of excitement near the kitchen table.

I waited another two hours, running through the plan in my head and making sure I had everything before leaving my apartment and entering Marcus's next door.

Getting into his place without being seen was a breeze. I searched his apartment for items that may prove useful for me and collected them. Sunglasses, extension cords, and a hammer. In the nightstand drawer, I found a gun and a switchblade.

The gun I ignored, but the pocket knife I grabbed. Tonight I was without my beloved razor blade and felt a little unbalanced. Having another small, sharp object gave me a sense of familiarity.

Returning to the front area, I dragged a chair closer to the door. I made sure to keep it far enough back so that the light from the hallway in the building didn't give me away when he opened it. I also made a few alterations to his layout.

The first thing I did was tie together three extension cords. One end I connected to the lower leg of his couch and the other to the bottom of a table across the room.

It was low enough that he definitely couldn't see it in the dark, but if he rushed at me, he would trip over it and increase his vulnerability.

Next, I looked around to ensure everything was to my

liking. Shelly left a few lamps on in her haste of leaving the apartment, and I turned them all off.

The last thing I did was use the hammer to break the light switch near his front door. With the exception of the light from the street lamps pouring in through the slightly opened blinds, it was completely dark in the apartment.

Luckily, the soft blue glow made it possible to see what I needed to. Now, all I had left to do was wait.

It seemed to take forever. I was tempted to abandon this waiting game and go out and find Marcus for myself when I heard it.

A rustling of keys at the door. After a moment, Marcus entered, and I caught a glimpse of his face and his unstable movements. My excitement surged.

Is Marcus drunk? Perfect.

Once inside, he closed the door and locked it. I heard him mumbling to himself.

"Stupid bitch left all the lights off. Shelly get your ass out here!" he yelled.

He swiped up and down on the wall, searching for the light switch.

"What the fuck?" he said to himself.

“Hello, Marcus,” I said to him.

CHAPTER NINE

"SHELLY HAS BEEN TAKEN CARE OF."

He was startled and reached for the light switch more frantically now. However, after a few seconds he abandoned the idea and spun around.

"Who's there?"

"Someone who wants some alone time with you."

This voice changer was fabulous. I loved it. I sounded like a badass mafia member or something.

"Where is Shelly?"

"Shelly has been taken care of."

I realized that my words implied that Shelly had been killed, and it worked out. This way, he was less likely to look for her. Clara better not ever tell me I'm not a good person.

"Shelly?" he yelled, not taking my word for it.

I said nothing, letting the absence of Shelly speak for itself.

"Who are you?" he asked.

"The wrong person."

"What the fuck is that supposed to mean?"

He placed a hand on the wall for balance, his intoxicated state clearly working against him.

"You've pissed off plenty of people, Marcus, but this time, you've finally pissed off the wrong person."

He took a step towards me.

"I wouldn't if I were you," I warn.

His voice sounded nervous when he said, "Listen, I've told Dino I will get him the money."

Dino? Well, well, looks like Marcus had someone slapping him around too.

I decided to let him keep thinking I was on the payroll of whoever had sparked this sudden, satisfying fear in him. It would make things easier.

I pulled the handcuffs from my pocket and tossed them to him. They landed in front of his feet.

"Get down on the floor and put these handcuffs on."

"Come on man, you don't have to kill me. I'll have the money by next week I promise... I give you my word."

I lifted the gun and repeated my demand. He did more begging until he heard me cock the gun, and that made him reluctantly comply.

After he was on his knees, and his hands were cuffed in front of him, I stood. I was careful as I moved towards him, trying to avoid tripping on anything while keeping my eyes on him.

He was watching me as well.

I couldn't quite see his eyes, but his head was turning, carefully following my movements. It was no big deal. He couldn't make out anything that revealed who I was.

The poorly lit living room, combined with my all-black gear, made me confident my identity was protected.

As I drew closer to him, my guard went up. This was where it got tricky. I'm sure Marcus was going to try and save himself, outsmart me, or fight back.

It would be perfect if he simply took his punishment like a man, but almost right on cue, he extended a leg to trip me.

I was prepared for his sudden movement, but miscalculated how far I stepped back and ended up bumping into a table. I fell to the floor and immediately rolled to the side, gripping the gun tight in case he was coming in my direction. I rose to my feet just in time to see Marcus standing as well.

However, instead of heading towards me, he ran further into the apartment.

Likely to the nightstand to get his gun. I didn't call out or even run after him because I knew what was coming.

Within the next second, Marcus tripped over my extension cord booby trap, slammed his head into the wall, and went down like he'd just been tackled by a linebacker.

Containing my laughter had to be one of the hardest things I'd ever done.

I walked over to him, he had rolled to his back, grunting and moaning his displeasures. He was wearing a black t-shirt that made it easy to see a tattoo of a lion on his arm. He was no fucking lion.

Tonight he was a kitten in a lion's den, and I was here to remind him of that. I pulled the blade out of my pocket and made a slice down the side of his arm, making the once powerful-looking tattoo a bloody mess.

He screamed, and I silenced him by placing one foot over his mouth. Sucks for him, I was certain these are the shoes I was wearing when I stepped in dog shit.

He shook his head violently and grabbed for my leg with his cuffed hands. I placed the gun on his temple, and like magic, he calmed down.

"Now that I have your attention," I said, "Let's try this again."

I instructed him to lay still while I checked his pockets. Then I placed a piece of tape over each eye and put the sunglasses on him.

His desire to fight back when I covered his eyes was so strong he was literally shaking, but he remained a good boy.

I think he could sense that I would end his life without hesitation.

I told him to stand, and he did so, leaning slightly to the left as he tried to straighten. Let's see, cut arm, possible pounding headache and vision blocked... yeah wavering on his feet sounded about right.

"You won't get away with this," he grumbled.

"Just stand there and look pretty. You'll be performing soon," I said.

I grabbed a medium size towel from his kitchen counter and draped it over his cuffed hands. Then I went to the door and unlocked it, sparing a few seconds to ensure the hall was clear. Everything looked good.

Marcus was still standing right where I left him. I saw his chest rising and falling quickly.

He better not piss his pants.

I walked over to him.

"The gun is aimed at you. Whenever you're feeling bold, I'm ready to shoot." He stiffened, but I grabbed his blood-free arm and gave it a pull. "Now, walk."

Marcus wasn't that much taller than me. I pegged him to be a few inches under six feet, which should make maneuvering him around pretty easy.

Then again, he might try to get cocky. For his sake, I hoped not.

Now that I had him where I wanted him, not ending his life was proving to be a challenge. I could pull this trigger and in a flash, rid the world of one more nuisance.

I decided to keep my distance in case he wanted to test me. I might fight pretty well, but I was not stupid. If I let this man get the upper hand, I was as good as dead.

I escorted him down the hallway and out a back entrance that was rarely used. The only person I passed leading Marcus away from the building was Gary the firebug.

He was setting papers on fire and stomping them out about 30 feet from the building.

Firestarter was far too engrossed in his own mischievous behavior to pay us any attention. I swear that little shit was going to burn down the whole building one day and if he did, I hoped he'd be the only one they couldn't rescue.

We finally arrived at our destination. Marcus almost stumbled over a rock, but caught himself at the last second. I continued checking the alley, and the only other person around was the one man that I came to see.

Joho faced us and grinned as we approached. He didn't bat an eye about being approached by two people in the dead of night. One of which was dressed in all black and holding a gun at the other who seemed to be in a vulnerable position.

The entire scenario warranted nothing more than an intrigued look from this sexual psycho.

I was simply grateful he was there. Joho was a big part of my plan. Without him, I'd have to take plan B, which was to abandon Marcus with a few gunshot wounds and let fate decide his outcome. A lot less intriguing, but justice would still be served no less.

Now that I think about it, shooting Marcus may still be on the agenda. We will see where the night takes us.

"You two looking for a fun time?" Joho asked.

I could smell the alcohol and grotesque body odor from here. I wondered when was the last time his body embraced water and soap.

"Not me, but my friend here is interested," I replied, shoving Marcus forward.

The voice machine was still doing a superb job of

distorting my voice. I had to remember to thank Nathan again for it.

I pulled the glasses from Marcus's face and yanked the tape from his eyes. I nudged the gun into his side, simply as a reminder, nothing more. I didn't want him to go getting all bold on me.

"He looks good," Joho said in a creepy voice.

I glanced at Marcus, who was utterly confused. From the expression on his face, I figured he was trying to piece things together and drawing a blank.

I'm sure he knew Joho, everyone did, but the reason he was here right now didn't seem to be clear.

Joho was licking his lips, reminding me of some type of lizard as his hand got closer and closer to his member down south.

My shoulders loosened slightly with relief. I was nervous as to whether or not this plan would work, but I think everything was going to be fine.

Why was I even worried? It's not like Joho was picky.

The last time I saw him, he was making love to a hole in the wall. Surely Marcus could be more useful than that. Yup, this was a brilliant idea. Turning the pimp into the trick, classic.

"What's going on?" Marcus asked, looking around. "Why am I here? Why the fuck is Joho here? What do you want?"

He seemed to be getting antsy. I pointed to the gun to remind him that this was my show, not his. He closed his mouth and swallowed.

"Good boy, Marcus," I said. "Now, since you are known for having a smart mouth, tonight you can use it to take care of Joho."

If I could have saved any image permanently in my mental database, it would have been the look on Marcus's face. He took an unsteady step back, visibly offended, shocked, and highly pissed.

"The fuck I am."

"This isn't a debate," I warned.

Marcus attempted to stand straighter and not look like the fuck boy he was about to be.

However, it was hard to look tough with your arm bleeding and your hands cuffed in front of you. If he tried to run, I was going to shoot him in the back.

I'd refrained from using the gun inside the building because it was too risky, but now that we were outside, he better tread carefully. I barely had any patience left, and after his next words, I ran out completely.

"Fuck you! I'm not going to do that. You may as well shoot me."

I aimed the gun at his leg and fired. The bullet ripped through his upper thigh, and he instantly dropped to his knees.

"Shit!" he yelled, grabbing the newly injured area. He rocked and cursed even more, but overall he was handling it better than I thought he would. Good for him.

"What were you saying?" I ask.

He didn't respond to me and that was not surprising. He was kind of preoccupied right now. What was unexpected was Joho's reaction. He laughed at Marcus and proceeded to pull out his dick.

Damn, Joho might have me beat in the insanity department, and that gave me a new respect for the man.

I squatted near Marcus being careful to avoid getting too close to Joho's joystick and said, "You're already in position, may as well start."

"Fuck you!" Marcus spat out. "You've shot me and now you think you're going to make me do this? If you're going to kill me," he said in a low voice, "then do it."

"With pleasure," I said.

He didn't have to ask me twice. I stood and aimed the gun at his head. I needed to get going anyway.

Someone may have reported that first shot. Police were likely to take forever getting their asses out here, but eventually, they would come.

Marcus stared straight ahead, determined to be strong and accept his fate, but I could see the fear creeping into his eyes. I didn't mind killing him, I simply hoped I wouldn't have to.

I wanted him to live with the memories of the night he exchanged places with Shelly.

I placed my finger on the trigger, but right before I pulled it, a new idea sprung to mind. Marcus was going to get a dose of a prostitute's life whether he liked it or not.

Joho's eyes were closed with his penis already fisted in his hand. He was pumping away a mile a minute, making odd squeaking noises. I hope it didn't take him much longer because I really did need to get the hell out of here.

"Hey, Joho."

The guy's eyes opened, and if possible, he appeared even more wild and crazed.

"You should finish on his face."

Joho didn't say anything, but the smile he released assured me that he heard me just fine. He took a sluggish step forward and closed his eyes again.

Having heard the conversation, Marcus was about to move when I gave him a hard kick to the face and he toppled over. He cursed again and reached for his head with his still restricted hands.

Tonight was certainly not his night. Looking up at Joho, he managed to mumble a threat.

"If you do this... I'll fucking kill you."

His persistence was adorable. He was in no condition to

do anything, but lie there and take it. Joho was in a world of his own and Marcus tried desperately to get out of the way.

He rolled onto his stomach and pushed himself up on one elbow. I watched him amused. He wasn't going any fucking where.

His sounds of distress could be heard easily when he placed too much pressure on his wounded leg, but knowing what was coming, he pushed through it and tried to get up anyway. I fired another bullet into his already damaged leg, and he collapsed onto his back.

This time the tough guy act melted away completely, and Marcus screamed.

His sudden vulnerability evidently pushed Joho over the edge because the man made a whistling noise and semen sprayed all over Marcus's face, shoulder and a little even landed behind his head.

I couldn't hold back this time. I laughed so hard that I had to lean over to catch my breath.

Joho was still masturbating with fury, and the voice changer made my laughter sound so much like a movie villain I laughed even harder.

Marcus was on the ground basically convulsing. He was spitting, cursing, and wiping at his face.

I finally collected myself, pulled out my phone and began snapping pictures of this unforgettable moment for insurance. I captured a few images that included Joho standing over him with his penis hanging like a lifeless worm. It was so nasty.

Yeah, I'm never having sex.

I heard sirens far off in the distance and knew that my time was up. Marcus had rolled to his stomach and was trying yet again, to get up. Before I made my quick exit I stepped on his back, pinning him to the ground.

"You have made worse enemies than Dino and tonight

was me playing nice. You have until the end of the month to get your shit and disappear. If you don't, not only will pictures of your steamy night with Joho be posted all around the city, your blood will paint these streets."

I undid the handcuffs, not wanting to leave behind anything that belonged to me. Even though Joho had nothing solid to report, I wasn't worried about him saying anything.

He'd probably describe me to the cops as some cool-looking action figure that helped him get his rocks off for the night.

The police were used to hearing him say crazy shit, so as far as he went, I was safe.

As for Marcus, his silence could also be expected. Not only was he not a favorable guy with the local authorities, he apparently was in deep with that Dino guy. Overall, the night went fantastic.

When the cops arrived they were going to find Marcus in a sticky situation, but I would be in the clear.

CHAPTER TEN

"WHAT DID THE POLICE SAY?"

A pounding headache jarred me out of my sleep. It came as no shock that I blacked out, again.

Across the room, Clara was pacing so frantically I was amazed the floor didn't have a hole in it.

"What's wrong, Clara?"

She stopped to glare at me and then started walking back and forth again.

Yup, somethings up. She was either worried, pissed, speechless, or all of the above.

However, if she didn't want to talk, I wasn't going to press. Besides, this ginormous headache was demanding all of my attention.

At this point, I should've seriously considered seeing a doctor, but I hated doctors.

They had too many questions and not enough answers, and what they didn't understand, they studied. I didn't want to be studied and given every experimental drug they could conjure up until a supposed cure was found.

I was studied long enough after the camp incident. My extreme behavior was both worrisome and intriguing to the staff at Field Grove Medical.

I was even given pill after pill to "fix" me, which never

worked. I let them believe it helped, but in all honesty, it only made me angrier.

Thank God Clara was around to keep me grounded because those pathetic excuses for doctors sure didn't.

I grabbed my bottle of water and ibuprofen from the side table. As soon as I poured a pill out into my hand, Clara decided to speak.

"The cops came by."

That explained it. Cops and Clara, not a good combo. I knew their mere presence stressed her to the max. Odd that I didn't hear them stop by.

Clara must have recognized the confused expression on my face because she answered my unasked question.

"You didn't know they came by because you were dead to the world. Another episode, right?"

I took my pill and shrugged.

"Sidney, why is it that every time you do something insane, I'm stuck trying to hold things together?"

There was nothing I could say; it was the truth. I made the mess, and when necessary, Clara cleaned it up. I went back into my mind to replay what I could remember from last night.

I came home, hid the handcuffs, knife, and gloves under a loose floorboard that I covered with a throw rug, and then went to the couch to calm my nerves.

Alright, I'm being dishonest, again. I went to the couch to replay the exciting events of the night. Everything played out so beautifully it felt magical.

Marcus hitting his head on the wall, the smell of blood when I sliced down his arm, and the anguish in his eyes after I shot him . . . both times.

I pulled out my phone and glanced at the pictures of a cum covered Marcus and laughed to myself. I even considered sending him a copy anonymously as a keepsake so that he could relive the night as often as I would.

Afterward, I planned to take a shower, but that was when it all went dark.

Either way, that was last night. At the moment I was wearing fresh pajamas, and I smelled like our lavender and vanilla body wash, but I didn't remember cleaning myself up at all.

"Sidney!" Clara yelled while snapping her fingers. "Focus. I know you like the blood and destruction but, you are out of control. They heard gunshots Sidney, gunshots! What the hell?"

"Gunshots aren't exactly rare around here and it doesn't mean that they suspect me."

"But they could and that's the point. I'm sure I don't even have to ask. You shot him didn't you?"

I took another giant gulp of water.

"If you know, why are you asking me?"

"At this point, I don't know. Hoping, wishing, praying," she paused to put her hands together, "that you aren't behind the drama this time."

My phone vibrated with an incoming call. It was Nathan. I wasn't going to answer it right now. I was not in the right frame of mind to talk to him.

"Was your plan to leave him there to die? Because he didn't."

"Yeah, I know. He was still kicking and crawling, quite well, last I saw him. So you can breathe easy. What did the police say?"

"What do you think they said? 'Your next-door neighbor was attacked and left in an alley not far from the building... know anything about it?'" Clara said, quoting the cops.

This was fascinating. Every time the police got involved, Clara usually dealt with it.

One day I'd like to be questioned. I pulled my hair up into a high ponytail, sat up straighter on the couch, and smiled. My phone chimed on the table with a text message from Cassie.

"What did you say?"

She placed her hands on her hips and gave me an irritated glare.

"I'll give you one guess."

"You said you'd ask the shooter about it when she wakes up."

Her eyes became mere slits.

“You never take me seriously. I have no idea why I even try. You’re loving this aren’t you?"

"Dodging the police? And the thrill of almost getting caught? Hell yeah."

"If you’re caught, I’m caught, remember? Besides, I'm doing the dodging while you nap."

I gave her my best puppy dog eyes.

"I can make it up to you with a game of chess," I said.

She visibly softened, and her eyes traveled in the direction of the chess game sitting on the shelf.

I noticed a tiny smile begin to form on the edge of her lips, and she said more to herself than to me, “I have a sister that kills for revenge. Other people write nasty letters, report you to the landlord for harassment, or even argue with you, but Sidney shoots you.”

I listened to her continue the Clara to Clara conversation and wondered where she was going with it.

“I may as well be talking to a brick wall for as much as she listens to me. But even though she is as unpredictable and lethal as anyone I know, I still love her. Maybe, I’m the crazy one."

“Maybe, you are,” I chimed in.

Clara looked at me and sighed. Then she came over and sat down next to me on the couch.

"You certainly are a challenge, but I can't stay mad at you. We take care of each other and even though I could never do what you do, I don't want to change you. It's because of you that Shelly is going to be okay and that makes me happy." She exhaled. "I simply told the police that I didn't know anything, but if something out of the ordinary comes to mind, I'll be sure to contact them."

I was a little disappointed.

"That's it?! No information about his condition, or what he told them? Nothing?

"Nope. I don't think the police share much with you, it's more about them getting answers. I did hear from Mr. Gregory that they took Joho into custody for questioning. Do you think we have anything to worry about?"

I gave it careful consideration. Taking Joho in was nothing more than standard procedure, I assumed. He couldn't identify me. Therefore, he certainly wasn't a reliable witness.

"No, we're good. I was careful in covering my tracks."

"Good. I was so nervous they would know I was lying."

"But you're a good liar, Clara."

"Only when I'm covering for you."

"Yeah, yeah, Little Miss Clara is always on the straight and narrow."

"You should try it sometime," she suggested.

"You never know I might surprise you one day."

"I won't hold my breath," she replied.

Then something strange happened. The lighthearted feeling in the atmosphere seemed to dissipate. It was replaced with a more serious, depressed one.

"Sidney, I haven't been feeling so well lately."

My heart began to pound. It was an unfamiliar feeling. I

rarely got nervous, and I couldn't recall the last time I was caught off guard.

"What's wrong?"

"I honestly don't know. I keep getting lightheaded, having trouble focusing, and on more than one occasion I've missed classes because I overslept."

I swallow slowly. This couldn't be happening, not now and not to Clara.

Was this payback for shooting Marcus... twice? I knew I should have only shot him the one time, but he wouldn't be still. Damn you, Marcus!

My heart ached for my sister. For her to admit that she wasn't feeling well meant that she had been holding it in for some time now. Clara wasn't a complainer. She was more of a container; a person that stored everything inside and tried to be strong, way too often.

"Why didn't you tell me?"

"I didn't want to worry you. I kept hoping it would get better. Kinda like you with your blackouts, but it seems to be getting worse."

My throat felt dry when I asked, "How do you feel right now?"

"A little weak to be honest."

"Do you want to see a doctor?"

She shook her head and pushed up her glasses. The dislike for doctors runs deep within us.

"I think I'll give it more time. If I don't get better I'll make an appointment."

"Are you sure? You know I'm willing to go with you. We can both be seen."

"No. Everything is fine. I probably need to drink more water or eat healthier. I'm sure it's nothing."

"Maybe you should take a break from school for a while

just to be sure. I'll continue to take care of everything for us and you can rest."

"Don't you mean you'll take care of *everyone*?" she said, trying to apply some humor to a tough conversation.

"Whatever works," I replied with a shrug.

She laughed and then got up.

"I guess I'll start right now. I'm going to take a nap. Are you going to be okay?"

I responded with the only truth I knew, "As long as you are."

"I'll deny it if you ever repeat this, but I'm glad that you gave Marcus a dose of his own medicine. Joho ejaculating on him was pure gold."

I threw my hands up.

"How in the hell do you always know details that I haven't shared with you?!"

"That's my secret," Clara said, giving me a wink. Then she blew me a kiss and headed to her bedroom.

I sat there, trying to figure out her spy secrets while waiting for my heart rate to return to normal from her outpour of health news. For a distraction, I picked up my phone and read the text message from Cassie.

She was asking me if I wanted to come in an hour earlier since I missed last night. I accepted the offer; it wasn't like I couldn't use more money, especially after this new development with Clara.

Clara. I thought

I felt sad again. I could not lose my sister; she was my everything. The world was too gloomy without her. I took a deep breath and put a pin in my worrying. Nothing was going to happen to Clara or me.

I considered returning Nathan's call. There was a possibility that talking to him could get my mind off things, but ultimately I decided not to. Instead, I would eat. Clara had left some yummy spaghetti in the fridge and come to think of it, I was starving.

I pulled out the bowl of spaghetti and poured myself a glass of juice when a knock at the door interrupted me. I opened it to see Barbara.

She watched me carefully. Presumably, studying my expression to gauge my mood.

"Hi Sidney," she finally said.

"Barbara," I responded, letting my displeased tone speak for itself.

"Clara called me. She was worried and needed someone to talk to. Is everything okay?"

I had no idea why Clara always confided in this woman.

"Everything is fine Barbara. No one needs you to practice your psychology on them today."

She stared at me.

“I would like to speak to Clara.”

“Too bad, she's asleep.”

“I could wait?"

“You could, but you won't. She needs her rest and I don't want any company.”

“I think you should let Clara decide that for herself.”

“I'm making the decisions right now, and I said you aren't needed.”

I tried to close the door, but she put her foot slightly inside to stop me. I looked down at it and then back up at her. She removed it and gave me an apologetic smile.

"Sidney, if you're in trouble, it's okay. I can help and I won't say anything."

“Barbara, I don't know what you and Clara have going on, but if you put your foot in my door again, the only person that is going to be needing help is you," I said and slammed the door shut.

On my way out of the building, as I was heading for work, I saw Mr. Gregory. He was taking his trash outside.

"Hi, let me get that for you," I offered, easily removing the bag from his grasp.

He looked up at me and smiled. I could see the top of his head. He was hunched over, and his salt and pepper colored hair was almost non-existent in the middle of his head.

"Sidney, thank you, dear. How have you been?"

"Great and yourself?"

"Oh, I've been better. Did you hear about the guy in this building that got attacked? I heard the gunshots, but I didn't think anything of it."

"Yeah I did, poor guy."

Mr. Gregory scoffed.

"Well, he wasn't exactly the nicest person. Always beating on his girlfriend and getting into trouble with the cops." He shook his head and gripped his cane tighter. "This neighborhood used to be so nice, now you don't know what to expect."

"That's so true. People are something else. Do the police have any leads?" I asked, hoping that he had some information Clara didn't.

"Not that I know of, but the girlfriend is nowhere to be found. I assume they will start with her," then he lowered his voice, "If she did do it I wouldn't be surprised. Serves him right for all he put her through."

"I agree. What goes around comes around."

"As it should." He touched my hand. "I'm just thankful there are still wonderful people in the world like you and your sister. Lord knows we need more of you."

My heart warmed at his words.

"Mr. Gregory, that has to be the nicest thing anyone has ever said to me."

"I know you had an emergency last night, everything alright?" Cassie asked while wiping down a vacant spot at the bar.

"I had some pressing matters to attend to, but everything has been sorted out now. Was it busy here?"

"Only in spurts. Nothing Grid and I couldn't handle, but we still missed you." Then Cassie snapped her fingers. "Oh yeah, the funniest shit happened last night. It took me a full hour to stop laughing."

"Oh wow, what happened?"

Cassie started laughing again. The story was clearly still too fresh and hilarious for her to resist.

"So get this. There was a group of guys at the bar that I served their first round of drinks and then went to tend to more customers.

Close to ten minutes later, one of the guys raised his hand for more service. I was still dealing with someone else, so Grid went to take care of it for me.

I overheard him telling the guy that his friends could have another round, but he couldn't because he already couldn't look at him straight. That's when the guy yelled, 'I'm cross-eyed you piece of shit!'"

The story caused me to laugh so hard that a few of the customers looked over at me, but I couldn't help myself, and neither could Cassie. She began laughing again as well.

"Damn, Grid had a bad night," I said.

"Yes. He was so embarrassed and couldn't apologize enough. Needless to say, they got free rounds for the rest of the night."

"It figures. As soon as I miss my shift something good happens."

"Don't worry, it's a bar. I'm sure more drama is coming soon."

She nudged me playfully with her shoulder and went to assist a customer. I headed to the back to restock some of the inventory we were getting low on. By the time I returned, a fresh crowd of loud-mouthed sports fanatics had entered the building. I did my usual flirting and engaged in idle chit-chat to keep the wallets open and the drinks coming. Before I knew it, I was an hour away from my shift ending.

My phone vibrated again in my pocket.

It was Nathan. I had completely forgotten to call him back.

"Hey babe, I'm sorry. It's been a busy day," I said.

"No worries, I figured as much."

"My shift ends in an hour. Do you mind if I give you a call back then?"

"Sounds perfect."

We ended the call just as another guy sat down at the far end of the bar. I pocketed the phone and walked over to him. At first, I couldn't quite see his face. He was looking down, giving the menu all his attention.

"What can I get you?" I asked.

That's when he looked up. I found myself momentarily speechless. It was Alexander Wright and sudden joy filled my spirit.

Could he be back for round two?

"Look at who we have here. You are a hard girl to track down, Sidney. Although, I have to admit, only emerging at night with the rest of the scum fits you."

"And I hear your limp fits you."

He gave me a smirk that made it clear he wanted to hurt me . . . real bad. He put the menu down and leaned closer.

"Good one. We'll see how much you're laughing once I'm done with you. There is no fucking way I'm letting you get away with what you did to me."

I licked my lips seductively and whispered, "But, I already got away with it."

"For now. However, once you and I spend a little time together, you're going to be begging for me to kill you."

I put my hand to my chest and feigned being flattered.

"Are you asking me out on a date?"

He hit the counter, and Cassie looked over, ready to grab her bat and come to my rescue. I raised my hand to let her know everything was good.

This asshole couldn't rattle me. I thought his attempt at being scary was actually sexy. He may have been pissed, and he may have been dangerous, but I didn't fear death... and I certainly didn't fear him.

"You're not safe. I'll be seeing you soon," he said, pointing at me before standing.

"Is that a threat?" I asked.

"It's a promise."

I watched him make his way towards the door, exiting the bar with a slight limp that made me giggle.

CHAPTER ELEVEN

"AIM FOR THE EYES."

I was ducking his blows, but not fast enough. He caught me a few times on my sides, and I barely felt it. I was concentrating, seeing him as the target I would inevitably have to face.

Maybe, it would be Marcus, or it could be Alexander, but it would be someone. I didn't expect that I could live my entire life making victims out of my enemies and get away unscathed.

If I was lucky enough to never meet a challenge I couldn't overcome, then great. In the meantime, I would keep training and building my strength.

I blocked Coleman's next blow and hit him with one of my own. It caused him to step back. I'd never landed a punch on him before.

"Exceptional job Sid! You're advancing pretty fast. Tell me the truth, have you been taking something?"

"You always ask me that, and the answer is always the same. I'm simply high on life."

"Damn, I keep hoping it's a yes so that you can give me some of it."

I laughed at his response. Coleman was a cool guy. He'd been training me in self-defense and general boxing for a few months now. He always pushed me to work harder, and I loved it.

"Well," Coleman said, "Since you've made victory and landed your first punch, let's call it a night."

"Aww come on, Cole. Just one more round?"

"I really wish I could Sid, but I got a hot date tonight. You always come so late in the day. Come earlier next time."

"If my schedule permits," I said, removing the gloves. "But I understand you wouldn't feel like a man tonight if a girl beats your ass in the ring before your date."

That got him. He paused and looked up at me.

"I'll bet you give your poor boyfriend a run for his money?"

I shrugged, and he caved.

"Alright, another 15 minutes, and we're done," he said.

I put my gloves back on and took my position, ready to battle.

After my time at the boxing club, I decided to go to the store. I'd finally convinced Clara to make her delicious stuffed bell peppers and rice recipe which meant I had to do my part by collecting the ingredients.

There weren't many people in the store, and I was able to take my time and browse aisles that I normally skipped over, such as the international food section and bakery.

It was 7 pm on a Friday night in the summer, and I was sure people had better things to do than grocery shop.

In a few hours, I would have something better to do as well. Cassie invited me to a party tonight, and I planned to attend. The last party I went to with her was wild.

I did so much dancing and singing with the live band that my feet and throat hurt for two days. It was awesome.

The crowd was energetic, loud, and lively. One guy even got so drunk he drove his car into the pool. No one was hurt, but the damages to that owner's property had to have been astronomical.

I slowed the cart as I approached the international aisle. Nothing looked too appealing, but I picked up the coconut water, willing to give it a try.

Next, I made my way to the bakery. I loved red velvet cake and chocolate chip cookies.

Today I bypassed those and picked up carrot cake. Like the coconut water, I'd never had this before, but for some reason, I was in the mood to try something different.

I grabbed a few more necessities such as bread, juice, bleach, and eggs and turned my cart in the direction of the checkout lane. My phone sprang to life in my pocket. Nathan again.

Shit, I once again forgot to call him back when my shift ended.

"Sidney!" he said when I answered the phone. His tone implied that something was wrong. I wondered what had him so shook.

"Yeah," I answered carefully.

"Why didn't you tell me someone got attacked near your building when we spoke yesterday?"

"Oh, that, it's no big deal."

"It's no big deal!? Sidney what if it was you that got hurt?"

"I'm sure that was simply some gang-related violence. Nothing for me to worry about."

I took a few steps forward. I was the next customer for checkout.

"Well, I don't like it. I worry about you and Clara. I would feel better if you came to live with me and if not with me," he said, cutting off my protest before it could escape my lips, "at least let me help you move to a safer area."

I wished it were that simple. I would love to move, it was Clara who wanted to stay close to what was familiar. I responded to Nathan with a genuine appreciation for his concern.

"You are so wonderful. Listen, I'm still going to decline to move in with you, but I'll talk to Clara about us moving to a safer neighborhood."

The relief in his voice is apparent.

"Thanks, Sidney. You have no idea how much better that makes me feel."

"Of course," I replied.

"Now that that's out of the way, what are you up to today?"

I approached the cashier and began unloading my cart. I tried to avoid buying too many items since I was walking home.

"Right now, I'm at the grocery store. Tonight I'm going to a party with Cassie."

"Sounds like a good time."

"I hope so. Want to hang out tomorrow?" I asked.

"I think I can squeeze you in. What do you have in mind?"

"Nothing major. Let's chill at your place."

"Alright, I'll pick you up around five."

I paid for my groceries and headed towards the exit. I was immediately hit in the shoulder with a stream of water as a group of teenage boys sprayed one another with their water guns. I laughed it off. It looked like they were really enjoying themselves.

I began to turn when I heard one of the boys yelling, "Stop it! I can't see you're hitting my glasses."

Three of the boys were attacking the fourth, and he

didn't seem too happy. He attempted to dodge them all, but they had him cornered and weren't letting up.

Now that I had a closer look, it was easy to see that he was smaller and possibly younger than the other three boys. They continued spraying him from every angle, laughing and calling him names.

He had a water gun too, but unlike theirs, it wasn't serving him any purposes. It was tucked under his arm while he used his hands to protect his face.

"Back off guys, I'm not playing anymore!" he yelled.

"Aww poor baby," one of them teased. "Jalen needs a break. That's not our problem."

They squirted him a few more times and then left him there. They ran close to 30 feet away to continue the water fight amongst themselves in the parking lot.

I walked over to him. He was slim and quirky looking.

"Hi, Jalen. You okay?"

"How do you know my name?" He asked, squinting suspiciously through water-covered glasses.

"I overheard one of your friends say it."

"Oh," he muttered, looking down. He then pulled off his glasses and cleaned them with the only dry patch he could find on his shirt.

"And they're not my friends."

"They aren't?"

"No, worse. They are my stepbrothers and I really don't think they like me. It's fine though, I just wish those assholes wouldn't gang up on me. They never give me a chance."

His posture was deflated and his lower lip was shaking. This obviously went deeper than simply losing the upper hand in a water fight.

"You know Jalen, sometimes the only reason people gang up on us is because they know they can?"

"I guess."

"How would you like to even the score?"

He slid his glasses back onto his face and looked up at me. I saw a glint of hope in his eyes.

"More than anything. But it's only me against three of them."

"That doesn't matter. Take them down one by one."

"How exactly am I supposed to do that?"

I put my three plastic grocery bags down and extended my hand.

"Let me see your gun."

He handed me the medium-sized, blue and green plastic toy with a puzzled look on his face. Unsnapping the blue latch at the top, I poured out all of the water.

"Hey!" he objected.

I ignored him and continued. Removing the bottle of bleach from my bag, I slowly poured it into the water gun. A little spilled down the side, and I wiped it away before replacing the latch and offering it back to him.

"Score evened," I said.

He took it, staring at the new turbocharged toy in disbelief before a slow smile spread across his face.

"But what if one of them gets hurt?" Jalen asked.

I wasn't convinced for a second that he actually cared. The tone in which he asked the question sounded more like an expected formality, not an honest concern. He was still staring at the gun like it was his new best friend.

"That's not your problem," I assured him.

"This would keep them off me."

My deed for the day was done. He could do with it what he pleased. I picked up my bags and turned to leave, happy that the kid finally seemed excited.

"Thanks!" he called out, "They won't see this coming!"

For his sake, I hoped he could fight or at least run fast

because his step brothers might beat his ass for what he was about to do.

Just in case he hadn't thought this through, I offered him an invaluable piece of advice, "Aim for the eyes kid."

I laced up my red boots and then walked to the bathroom to style my hair and apply some glossy wine-colored lipstick.

"Don't you look sexy?" Clara said, approaching the bathroom door.

"Thanks. I do alright, how was your day?"

"Quiet and unadventurous, just like I like it."

"Good."

I smacked my lips together a few times and then winked at my reflection. I looked totally hot.

"Where are you off to?"

A party with Cassie, you want to come?"

"Nah, I'll live vicariously through you. Besides, I went by early this morning and visited grandma. I'm done with the outdoors for today."

"How is she?"

"She's okay. I think her memory is getting worse, though."

That definitely brought down my good mood a few notches. I knew memory loss came with old age for many, but it was still horrible.

I'd try to get by next week and visit her. I added another layer of gloss to help shake my thoughts of sadness and get back into the mindset of sexy.

"Oh, by the way, thanks for the coconut water and carrot cake."

I stopped admiring my reflection.

"Umm, you're welcome."

"You got those for me, right?"

"Not necessarily. I mean you're more than welcome to them, but I was simply trying something new.

"Oh. I love carrot cake and haven't had coconut water in years. I used to drink it when I was studying for tests in high school."

"That's funny. I never knew that and here it was I thought I knew everything about you."

Clara smirked.

"Imagine that, Sidney doesn't know everything."

I put my lipgloss down and gave Clara my full attention.

"How've you been feeling? Have the weak and dizzy spells gotten any better?"

"Slightly. It was a good idea to take a semester off. My concentration was getting horrible and my grades were even starting to slip."

"Oh Clara, I didn't know it was that bad. I'm so sorry. I hate that you're going through this. I wish there was something I could do. Delaying your degree has to be hard on you."

"It is, but I'll be okay. Thank you for always keeping me going, Sidney. I don't think I tell you that enough."

I waved her off. I didn't need appreciation for doing for her what she would so easily do for me. I grabbed a bobby pin and fastened it to a small section of hair that kept falling into my face.

"What about you? Have you been staying out of trouble? You haven't killed anyone lately have you?

"Nope. I've been making progress."

I blew myself a kiss in the mirror.

"Progress, huh? What about your blade?"

I moved it forward with my tongue and held it in between my teeth.

"I only have it for protection, nothing more," I said after I shifted it back into place.

I picked up my phone, snapped a quick selfie, and sent it to Nathan. A few seconds later, my phone vibrated with an incoming text, but it wasn't from Nathan, it was from Cassie letting me know she was outside.

I did one final check in the mirror and turned to my equally gorgeous sister.

"I'll have enough fun tonight for us both."

The party was at an abandoned warehouse in a classier part of town. Classier being the operative word since it was not difficult to find neighborhoods that were better than mine. There had to be hundreds of people here enjoying themselves like there was no tomorrow.

"Let's go dance, little doll," Cassie shouted over the noise.

She grabbed my hand and pulled me into the crowd. We both immediately started jumping, shaking, grinding, and twisting our bodies to the music. Cassie was such a great dancer, better than me, but I had a few moves I'd mastered pretty well.

We danced to several songs before the desire for a much-needed break set in.

"I'm going to go grab a drink, you want one?"

"Hell yeah! Bring me something strong," she said, still moving her body to the beat.

I located a table full of drinks. Everything from bottles of beer to soda to water and even plastic red cups with a dark brown liquid inside sat on the table, ready to quench everyone's thirst. I decided on the beer because I wouldn't dare take a chance on those 'red cups'.

I returned to Cassie, making my way through the crowd, stopping to flirt with a few handsome guys on the way.

We drank our beers, danced a little more, and then parted ways.

A tattoo artist was doing free tattoos in the back of the warehouse, and Cassie had a new skeleton tat she just had to have.

We planned to meet up at the drink station in an hour, and I was officially on my own. I had plenty to keep me busy.

I danced with a few guys, watched and mentally bid on the winner of several of the fights that erupted, then took a break in a corner to people watch.

That's when I noticed something I didn't like. I was sipping my second beer of the night when I saw a guy talking to a girl near the drink area.

The girl leaned in to hear something he was saying. He had one hand on her shoulder, but the other was pouring something from a little bottle into a red cup.

See! No one can trust what's in the red cup.

I straightened and put my beer down. The guy placed the tiny bottle back on the table and discreetly pushed it behind a case of beer.

Finally, having heard what the guy said, the girl laughed and playfully hit him on the shoulder. He reached for the cup and passed it to her, then picked up a second one on the opposite side for himself.

Fuck!

I couldn't get to her fast enough, and the girl took a sip.

As I closed in on the couple, the guy put his cup down, but the unlucky girl was still holding on to hers, completely unaware of the danger she was in. I made a beeline in their direction to knock it out of her hand when I saw an opening behind the table.

I started dancing and working my way back there instead. I located the short bottle right behind the case of beer where he'd placed it. I picked it up, giving it a quick inspection.

It had no label, and the liquid inside was clear. I slid it into the back pocket of my skirt. Then I grabbed a bottle of beer, opened it, and poured half of it out.

Getting closer to them, I overheard the girl saying, "You are so funny."

"I've been told that a time or two," he said. "But it's easy when I'm in the company of such a beautiful girl."

She giggled, and I intentionally bumped her shoulder so hard the drink slipped out of her hand and splashed on the floor.

"I am so sorry," I said.

As soon as she began to tell me that it was no big deal, my eyes went wide with surprise.

"Oh my goodness it's you!"

The girl looked puzzled. I snapped my fingers and pointed at her.

"You're that famous singer."

"Huh? I'm not—"

I stepped closer and slightly in between her and the predator guy, then faced him.

"Doesn't she look like the girl?"

He had the most baffled expression on his face, and I pressed on.

"You know the girl? The girl that sings the 'I love you' song. Come on, look at her! Don't you see it?" I nudged him towards her.

As he was leaning closer to the girl and shaking his head, trying to understand who the hell I was talking about, I pulled the mystery bottle out of my pocket and emptied the contents into his cup.

"Um, I'm sorry I don't know who you're talking about," he said.

I shook my head and sighed.

"Damn, you know what? Maybe she doesn't. I think I've probably had way too much to drink. I'm just so excited tonight. I'm celebrating my engagement!"

"Oh wow!" the girl said, her eyes filling with excitement. "Congratulations!"

She looked down at my hand for a ring, and I tossed out another lie as easily as I took my next breath.

"Shawn is broke as hell. He can't afford the ring right now, but I told him a ring means nothing when two people love each other like we do."

The girl touched her chest and nodded. The guy rolled his eyes, picked up his drink, and took a gulp. Thank God. He just made my next move a lot easier.

"Hey," I said, fully facing him. "Do you mind doing a quick toast with me? I promise I'll be out of your sight afterward."

"Why the hell not," he replied with a shrug.

"To life and love," I said, raising my bottle. "Here's hoping that everyone gets exactly what they deserve."

"Odd toast, but I'll drink to that."

He took another giant swallow of his drink while I consumed more beer. I coaxed him into finishing his whole cup as I finished my beer, and then as promised, I was out of his sight, but he wasn't out of mine.

I staggered away to a tall stack of boxes off to the side and stood behind them, watching for whatever was in the mystery bottle to take effect. The minute it hit him that something wasn't right, I could tell.

He went from talking to suddenly holding up a hand and then rushing away. When he disappeared into the crowd, I went back to her.

"Oh, hi again!" she said cheerfully.

"He spiked your drink," I responded, cutting to the chase.

"Huh?"

"The guy you were talking to. He spiked your drink . . . with this."

I pulled the small bottle from my back pocket and showed it to her.

"What? . . . I . . . I don't understand."

Damn, she was slow. No wonder he picked her. I gave it another shot, explaining what I saw and how I gave him a dose of his own medicine. When I was finished, her eyes filled with tears.

Oh shit, she's a crier. Why me?!!

"Thank you so much! I don't know what I would have done if you weren't here."

"Just watch yourself from now on. People can't be trusted. Do you feel okay?"

"Yes, I feel fine. I only took a tiny sip when he gave it to me. I honestly really don't like alcohol."

"Good, maybe you should stick to bottles of water from now on."

"I definitely will. Thank you again," she said, grabbing my hand. "You saved my life."

I smiled at her. I'd just saved a life instead of taking one; look at me making progress.

CHAPTER TWELVE

"YOU'RE SUCH A FREAK."

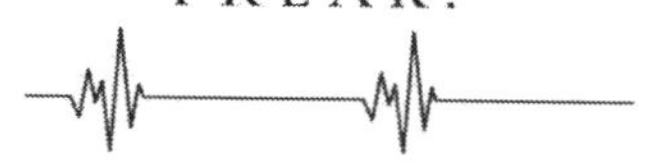

My eyes were glued to the TV, and Nathan's arm was around me. It was so amusing that he thought he was making me feel safe and protecting me from the scary parts.

If anything, these movies were giving me ideas. How come I never thought about putting a dead body in a barrel of acid?

I'd surely need a car first and a house as well. Can't be dragging people to the car with a building full of nosy neighbors peeking out their windows. I sighed and settled into his arm.

Oh well, it was probably not very effective at eradicating evidence anyway.

I'd need way too much of it to soak a body in, and what would happen if some of it splashed on me?

That would mean I'd also need a protective suit. Ugh! Yes, acid would be a total headache.

Nathan embraced me tighter, and I cleared all thoughts of body elimination methods and re-focused on the movie.

The killer chased the woman around the house as she screamed, cried out, and tripped over almost everything in her house, but in the end, he caught her.

Oh yeah, this is the good part.

"You okay? Is this too scary?" Nathan whispered.

"No, I'm fine, it's only a movie."

The killer brought down the knife and stabbed the woman repeatedly, and my mind began to wander again.

The last thing you heard before the scene ended was her scream. That part about certain movies always annoyed me. I wanted to see the entire murder happen.

I needed to know how long the victim screamed. Was it until the knife was buried into their body the second time? Third? or fourth?

Expectantly, some victims would last longer than others, and of course, this was fiction but all sources of research helped.

I rolled my eyes and picked up more popcorn. The next scene was of a couple heading for a vacation at the same cabin the woman in the scene before died in.

I already knew how this movie was going to end, so I mentally checked out again and considered how much traffic the bar might have tonight. It was Saturday, so things might be fast paced.

My thoughts were interrupted by Nathan tilting my face to his and kissing me. It was unexpected, but I fell in line quickly. I enjoyed kissing him.

His lips were soft, and he knew how to use just enough pressure to make the butterflies feelings appear.

"I've been wanting to do that all night," he said, breaking off the kiss.

"What stopped you?" I asked.

"You seemed a little preoccupied."

"Yeah, I have things on my mind."

"Anything you want to share?"

"I'm worried about Clara. She hasn't been doing so well."

"Sorry to hear that, is there anything I can do?"

"You're already doing it."

He took my hand in his and caressed it.

"You're a wonderful sister, Sidney. There is no way that most people would do what you do. You love her, protect her and even put her needs ahead of your own."

I could agree with everything he said, but I also did those things because I had no choice. Clara was a worrier by nature, so I often sheltered her from the bad. It rarely worked, but I still tried.

For instance, that run-in I had with Alexander at the bar hadn't left my lips. If Clara got wind of it, she'd ban me from leaving the house ever again.

Nathan and I spent the rest of the movie in silence. The couple didn't survive. No surprise there, but neither did the killer.

Now that's something you don't see often.

Overall it was a good movie, and it sparked a question in my mind that I shouldn't have asked Nathan, but I simply couldn't resist.

"Hey Nathan, what would you do if you found out I was a murderer?"

He laughed and started cleaning up our mess. I got up to help him.

"What's so funny?" I asked, picking up the bucket of popcorn.

"That question. Even though I know it's hypothetical I couldn't imagine you killing a fly."

"Okay, but play along anyway."

He put his soda can down and watched me carefully.

"Hmm, if I found out you were a murderer I wouldn't do anything."

"Yeah right, why is that?"

"Because you're too cute to turn in to the police," he said, pulling me close to him.

I laughed and pushed away from him. Looking into his eyes, I said, "I'm serious."

He exhaled.

"I don't know Sidney. What would any man do if he found out the woman he loved had killed someone?"

"Run for the hills?" I offered.

"Or I'd probably look the other way or rationalize it until I couldn't anymore I guess."

"But you wouldn't freak out?"

"Yeah I would, but considering the why, would make a difference."

"What if I did it merely because I could."

"Then I'd get you the best doctors in the world."

He pulled me to him again, and this time I didn't push away. It felt nice in his arms.

My head on his chest, listening to his strong, steady heartbeat. He kissed the top of my head and whispered into my hair, "Luckily for me, I'd never have to worry about my angel doing such horrible things."

I hugged him tighter.

"Lucky you," I said back.

Nathan took me to work the next night, and I was so grateful. I had worn myself out in the boxing ring earlier that day and wasn't in the mood to walk or pay for an Uber.

When I was exiting my apartment building on the way to Nathan's car, I noticed that Marcus's place was still quiet.

There were rumors in the building that he wasn't coming back at all, and I felt elated that he had heeded my warning.

Best of all, it didn't even take until the end of the month.

People really could surprise you when there were bullets involved.

"Are you free tomorrow, around 5:30?" Nathan asked, pulling up to the bar.

"I should be."

"Cool. I want to take you to this Japanese restaurant where you sit on the floor and eat."

"A new experience sounds lovely."

"I knew you'd say that. Have a good day at work, alright?"

"I will."

I gave him a quick kiss and went inside, heading straight for the bathroom to tie up my t-shirt so that my stomach was exposed; I had to make it enticing for the tips.

I pulled my covered razor blade from my back pocket and inserted it into my mouth.

Instantly I feel back in my element, safe, protected, and whole. I'd been meaning to buy something else that I could keep with me for protection, however, I hadn't made the time.

I loved my blade, and I wasn't looking to trade it in, but an additional weapon that wouldn't require me to get so up close and personal with an attacker to defend myself was smarter. I'd make it a priority next week.

After a few hours of work, I was grateful that my shift tonight had been easy, but busy so far.

Not only did I make tons of tips. I was able to pocket a lot of extra cash in the process. I looked over at Cassie and noticed the new skull tattoo she got at the party. When I saw it that night, it seemed smaller.

Now it appeared to cover most of her lower arm.

I walked over to her after placing a client's drink on the bar.

"Why does your tattoo look bigger?"

Cassie blushed and bit her lower lip.

"Because Metro added to it."

"Metro?"

"That's the tattoo guy from the party. I gave him my number, but I didn't think he would call. However, he did the next morning. We met for breakfast, one thing led to another and before I knew it he was marking my body as his in all sorts of ways."

"You're such a freak," I said, shaking my head.

One of the regulars called her over, and she held up one finger to him.

"Don't worry little doll, you'll get there one day," she said with a wink before strutting away.

I doubt it. I thought to myself.

It wasn't long before my shift was over. I couldn't wait to turn in for the night. I took my usual stroll home, stopping by the ATM to deposit my cash.

This neighborhood may not be the best, but it was certainly convenient, for me at least.

Every place I frequented, such as the bank, park, grandma's house, my job, and the grocery store, were within walking distance.

With the exception of grandma's house, I passed all of them on my route home.

When I got closer to the area I normally noticed Joho in, it was empty. I knew for a fact he was already released from the police station, which meant he was probably getting lucky a few streets over.

He was known to have several spots where he could get his grinding on.

Behind me, I suddenly heard footsteps. I stopped, and so did the echoing sound of shoes hitting the pavement. The next logical thing to do was to steal a glance behind me, which was what I did, but no one was there.

This isn't good.

I knew that I wasn't crazy. However, reflexively, I began questioning myself.

Was my mind playing tricks on me, or was someone truly following me? Do I know them? Was it Alexander? Marcus? Someone else?

My guard was now raised. Someone was definitely toying with me. My suspicions were confirmed when a man I'd never seen before covered my mouth and nose with a damp rag.

I didn't have time to blink, scream or land a damaging blow to his body, but I didn't panic, and as I trained myself to do long ago, I held my breath.

He lifted me into the air effortlessly, and I kicked, clawed, and grabbed onto his wrist in an attempt to break free . . . or at least make it look like I was.

You see, I couldn't win this fight. The man was two, possibly even three sizes bigger than me, and had me in a position that offered minimal advantages being this close.

The harder I fought, the more air I would lose, and the chances of me inhaling whatever was on that rag would soar. So instead, I fought a little longer and slowly lessened my resistance until I was no longer resisting at all.

I slumped in his arms, and after a few seconds, he released me, and I cautiously took a slow, measured inconspicuous breath.

He hoisted me up over his shoulder, and I tightened my jaw to ensure I did not swallow my razor blade.

Believing me to be unconscious, he carried me what I counted to be 30 steps and then stopped. I heard a car unlocking, and I slid my eyes open just a pinch. His shoes were white and red, with a star symbol on them. A second pair of shoes stepped into my vision.

"This was easier than I thought," the guy holding me said.

"I told you it would be a piece of cake," the other replied.

I closed my eyes quickly as I felt the one holding me shift his weight. After removing me from his shoulder, I was placed on a hard, carpeted surface that smelt like beer.

How did you like that? Start your day at your own home, but end it in the trunk of someone's car.

CHAPTER THIRTEEN

"WAKE UP, BITCH!"

I'd never been in a trunk before, and the ride was bumpy as hell.

I had to spread my legs several times to brace myself if I wanted to avoid rolling into something lumpy and round on my left.

Hmm, no bound hands or feet, and they didn't even check my pockets to remove my cell phone.

This definitely screamed amateur and that little revelation pointed to Alexander.

"Well, he did promise world-class retribution," I mumbled to myself.

I rolled my eyes in the dark, cramped space coming to the exciting conclusion that this may not be a wasted night after all. I was long overdue for some action, and who better to take it out on than the man who thought he was invincible.

My only question was who was the hired muscle? Or were they friends of his? Did they always do this sort of illegal, unethical crap for him? Probably so, he did have deep pockets from what I'd heard, and for the right price, people lost all morals.

The driver made a sharp turn, and a hard object hit my foot, causing me to wince.

Dammit. I'll bet that did some damage to my shoe.

I reached down to touch the object.

Tracing my fingers over it, it seemed to be a . . . a barbell? I repositioned my body and tried to lift it. I had no luck because it was heavy as shit.

There went the idea of using that as a weapon; it would have been impossible to gain enough leverage to lift it and land a solid blow at this angle. I possibly had three men to outsmart.

Better come with something a little more unexpected.

I pulled my almost dead cell phone out of my pocket. I wasn't planning on using it right now, but I'd like to have a working phone when it came time for me to leave this place.

Then it hit me. I might not leave this place. Well, I guess in that case, the almost dead battery really wouldn't matter.

I wasn't in the car much longer before it came to a complete stop. The ride didn't seem to take long, but I knew for sure we were out of my area.

I should have timed it.

I heard two voices near the trunk, and I listened closely. Their voices were a bit muffled, but I could mostly make out what they were saying.

"I don't know what she did to him, but he is pissed."

"Oh shit, you didn't hear? She's the reason he had to sit out the football season. Everyone was talking about it at the party a while back.

No one saw who did it and all Alexander told the paramedics and cops was that some girl attacked him."

"But if he doesn't know who did it, then why is he so sure this is her?"

The guy chuckled and said, "Oh he remembered her, he just told them that because he wanted to find and deal with her himself."

"Damn. What exactly did she do to him?"

"Razor blades man. Embedded in his sides and legs."

"You're fucking kidding! He's going to kill her."

I heard a third voice pour into the conversation. It was deeper and colder, absolutely Alexander.

"Is she knocked out?" he asked one of the guys.

"Sleeping like a baby."

"Not for long," Alexander said.

I heard the trunk make a popping sound, and suddenly it was open. My eyes were still closed, but that warm breeze from the serene night air felt heavenly. I hadn't realized how stuffed it felt in here until now.

"Jacob! Why the fuck didn't you tie her up?!" Alexander exclaimed.

Exactly!

I had to agree with Alexander on this one. Apparently he had more brains than I gave him credit for. I hoped he wasn't paying this guy.

"Relax man, she's no threat. I made sure she was knocked out."

I could hear the irritation in his voice when Alexander said, "Pete, take her inside. I don't want Jacob fucking anything else up."

Pete, presumably, grabbed my arm, not too gently, and yanked me upward. It took all my self-control not to hit him in the throat as he slid the other arm underneath me and lifted me from the trunk.

Once inside, Alexander instructed Pete to check my pockets and then tie me up. My cellphone and wallet were removed before I was strapped into the chair.

One of my legs was tied to each of the chair legs, a rope was pulled around my waist and tied to the back of the chair, and my wrists were bound together in front of me.

Shit. Getting out of this was going to be a challenge.

Nevertheless, Alexander was truly impressing me with his hostage skills. I wondered if he'd done this before. Maybe we had more in common than I'd imagined.

Regardless, my options for defending myself and escaping were vanishing quickly. I still felt calm though.

He was going to fuck up, and when he did, I would be ready.

I slumped in the chair and listened. The floor creaked as they talked.

Where in the hell was I?

"What are you looking for Alex?" Pete asked.

"Something to make her stay a little more exciting," he replied in a sadistic tone.

"Oh, okay. Well, if that's all you need Jacob and I are going to get back to the campus. I have a major test tomorrow and I'm already on academic probation."

"I don't give a shit about your problems, Pete. This isn't a counseling session. The money I promised will be deposited into your account on Monday. You can tell Jacob the same."

He should have kept his money; those idiots did a horrible job.

"Alright, see you later," Pete said. From the sound of it, I assumed he began to walk away but then stopped.

"By the way, you got any more of that stuff that makes the girls play nice so we can have some fun? I have a new freshman I've been eyeing and invited her to the party next month."

A date rape drug, I'll bet. Those assholes.

"No, I sold the last of it two days ago. I'll get some more soon."

"Cool, check you later, man . . . oh and have fun with her, she's sexy."

I heard the door close, and Alexander's footsteps drew

closer to me. From the clarity in his voice, he must have been standing right in front of me.

"Look at you now. You think you're so special and so smart don't you?"

I almost said yes, but at the last second I caught myself. I was supposed to be knocked out, but the guy had to know it was hard to resist someone boosting your ego.

"Well, I'm going to show you you're nothing."

He walked away, and the floor once again creaked repeatedly in protest. I opened my eyes a little. The floors were rustic and dusty. I heard Alexander returning and closed my eyes again.

"Wakey, wakey bitch!" Alexander said, as he waved something so strongly scented under my nose I didn't have to fake my reaction.

I jumped back, or as far back as I could while restrained in a chair.

It must have been smelling salts. Those things were so powerful they could wake up the dead.

I looked around the place, letting my eyes fully adjust to the light, and asked in a small voice, "Where am I?"

"At your final destination."

I scanned the room. I was in a cabin, an unkempt cabin at that. Although it was pretty much fully furnished. It looked old and deserted.

Cabinets were hanging off the hinges, there was a small hole in the floor over in the corner, and all of the lights in the seven bulb fixture hanging above our head were all blown out except three.

Luckily, it still provided enough light for me to see all I needed to.

My eyes landed back on his. Oh, he was pissed. I'd give it to him, he was starting to make me a little nervous, but I was also fascinated.

He obviously had kidnapped someone before; he seemed too comfortable with it. However, was he a killer? Hmmm, I wasn't sure.

I continued questioning him, with panic and despair lacing my voice as I glanced around the room, checking for weapons.

There was a knife on the table not too far from me and a giant glass unit a few feet directly behind where he was standing.

"But why are you doing this? I'm sorry about what I did to you. Please just let me go and I won't tell anyone about this. I swear."

"It's too late now. You should have thought about that before you messed with a man that has as much power as me."

'Power?' Careful Alexander, your arrogance is showing.

"What are you going to do to me?" I asked.

He looked me over slowly and then glanced back at the knife on the table.

"That's none of your concern. After all, whatever I want, I get, and no bitch is going to stop me." He licked his lips, and then looking down at my breasts, he said, "I'll let you guess what I want first."

He clearly had a problem with women, and that was my in. I decided to switch tactics.

"Do you want a limp in your left leg to match your right?" I asked, smiling.

He slapped the shit out of me for that one. But I braced myself for it seconds before his hand connected to my face. Still, that hurt!

Nothing like the punches I got at the boxing ring when I was wearing a face pad for protection.

My vision blurred, and I momentarily saw stars, but I

welcomed the pain. It kicked my adrenaline up, and it proved that he was angry. I liked seeing him angry.

Almost as much as I like seeing him hurt.

"You bitch! You will not talk to me like that."

"Why not, does it prevent you from getting it up?"

His next hit I didn't brace for as well, and it drew blood.

"Don't test me!" he screamed and paced the floor.

He was balling up his fists then releasing them repeatedly while muttering curses.

My only saving grace was that he did not connect with the side my razor blade was on. My head was hanging low as blood leaked out, and I took that second to let the tiny covered blade fall out of my mouth. It landed on my upper thigh, easily concealed by my bound hands.

I coughed and spit out more blood while discreetly grabbing the blade and closing my fist around it.

"You think you're something? Resisting me! Questioning me! No one questions me!"

He picked up something off the table and came towards me with it. I was still looking down, and he grabbed a handful of my hair and pulled so hard I'm certain he ripped some out.

He placed the knife at the side of my face.

"I was going to have some fun with you before I brought on the pain, but since you can't keep your mouth shut. I think I'll start with the pain first."

Using light pressure, he dragged the knife down my face. I squeezed my eyes closed and tried to pull from his grasp to no avail."

"Got anything else you want to say, slut?"

I nodded my head.

"You better kill me because over my dead body is the only way you're going to have me, lover boy," I said with a chilling smile, and I meant it.

He would either back down or be pressured into wanting to prove himself. My life depended upon it being the latter. I needed this bastard to untie me.

Instead of gaining instant freedom, the remark earned me yet another strike.

It packed so much force it caused the chair to topple to the left, bringing me down with it. I tried to throw my body in the opposite direction to avoid hitting my head against the floor, and it worked, mostly.

My shoulder caught the brunt of it, and like the blows to my face, it left a searing pain behind that made me momentarily light-headed. Alexander grabbed my hair again and used it to pull me and the chair back up.

"Oh, we will see about that."

He leaned down and began cutting through one of the knots that connected my leg to the chair, and I got excited.

It worked!

And here it was, I thought I didn't give him enough credit in the intelligence department.

He was a fucking moron, and that weakness was about to cost him his life. Death was coming for him today, and I would be the one to open the door.

While he freed my first leg and then the second, I used the distraction to remove the protective plastic from my blade. I slowly turned it using my thumb and pointer finger so that the sharp side was facing out.

He stood and started cutting through the rope around my waist. I was mentally calculating the distance between him and that glass case.

I was a little dizzy, but I could gather up enough strength to make the connection.

Once I was freed, he grabbed my arm and pulled me to my feet.

"You are about to pay for that smart mouth of yours."

"Not before you do," I spat back.

He wasn't ready on any level for what happened next. My movements were quick and precise when I dragged the blade down the left side of his face, splitting his eyelid and possibly even his eye in half.

His howl of pain was cut short when I kicked him with all the force I could manage.

He collided with the giant glass unit just as I'd hoped, causing it to shatter into a million pieces. I stared in awe as his body collapsed to the floor amidst a blanket of glass.

"Beautiful," I said.

Hands still bound, I picked up the knife and walked over to him. He was in bad shape. His face was so bloody I could barely make out his features, and pieces of glass were buried all over his body.

However, none of them mattered as much as the giant piece in his neck. He reached for it, and I kicked his hand away.

"No, No, No," I said, wagging a finger.

He was too weak to do much at all. His body was jolting from the pain, and I suspected he was dying. I picked up the knife and held it above him.

“Let me help you."

I buried the knife into him several times before he went completely limp.

Not ready for the fun to be over, I continued to stab him. The exhilaration and thrill of such a savage act satiating my dark side in ways words can’t describe.

I eventually tore myself away from the delicious pleasure and stood to catch my breath. I looked down at Alexander, or what used to be Alexander.

Yup,. he’s dead.

Blood was everywhere, and my hands, clothes, and even shoes were covered. I went back to the chair and sat down.

Carefully, I positioned the knife in-between my legs and rubbed the ropes over the blade until my hands were free.

A cell phone vibrated on the table, and it wasn't mine. My phone rested a few inches away, probably as dead as Alexander was. The display read Jacob.

"Sorry, Jacob. Alexander has checked out, permanently."

I had to get cleaned up and get the hell out of here. I went over to the sink and washed off as much blood from my hands, face, and neck as I could.

I even tried to rinse some of the blood from my shoes, but that proved pointless because on the way by Alexander, I kicked him, angry that he messed them up in the first place.

There was a mirror over the table in the corner, and I used it to check my work. As far as I could see, my face was clear of any blood streaks.

Afterward, I picked up my cellphone and wallet.

As I suspected, my phone was dead. I put them both into my back pocket, then searched the floor for my razor blade, and its cover.

Once found, I shoved it into my pocket as well. I also collected the knife and ropes used to restrain me and then meticulously checked the area again.

In the closet, I found a big black jacket and pulled it on. It landed slightly above my knees and covered up enough of the blood on my clothes so if someone saw me, I wouldn't stand out.

As far as my shoes went, if questioned I'd just have to say I was playing in paint.

I faced the room again. I'm sure there was tons of evidence left, but I did the best I could. If they wanted proof of his murder, I was sure they would find it.

Plus, as soon as the police put pressure on Jacob and Pete, they were going to be singing like canaries about the girl they kidnapped for Alexander, just to clear their names and strike a deal.

I needed to get as far away from here as possible while I still had the chance.

I exited the shabby-looking cabin through the back door using part of the jacket to turn the knob. I saw Alexander's car parked on the side, but I don't even consider it an option for escape.

Getting rid of a car would be too much of a headache.

I decided to walk for a while and enjoy the night air. There weren't many houses around, and it was deathly quiet out here.

The thought was so fitting it made me smile. I stopped near an area of cluttered trees and bushes to dispose of the knife and ropes.

I dug a little with my hands so that the items weren't simply sitting right on top and then covered it with the dirt and some shrubs and sticks for additional concealment. I probably walked close to an hour before I reached a gas station.

As I got closer to the building, I pulled my hair out of its ponytail and let it fall down so it would be difficult to get a clear view of my face on camera. I went inside to ask the cashier if they could call me an Uber, and within two hours, I was home and showered.

I tied my clothes, jacket included, up in a bag and fell onto the couch. I was exhausted.

Carrying out my civic duty to end Alexander's life may have been worth it, but it had taken a lot out of me.

All I needed was to close my eyes for a second and . . .

I woke up coughing and disoriented. Smoke had filled the apartment, and there was pounding at the door.

"SIDNEY!"

I heard someone calling my name through the door. I stumbled over, still coughing and confused.

What the hell is going on?

I opened it and barely saw Nathan in the smoke-filled hallway. He was covering his nose and mouth and rushed in.

"There is a fire in the building and I need to get you and Clara out."

I looked at him perplexed.

Fire? But I heard no alarm, and everything seemed so blurry. This must be a dream.

His words somehow weren't sinking in. My head was pounding, and my body felt so heavy.

"Is Clara here?" he asked.

"Clara?"

I repeated her name and looked towards the bedroom.

"I'll get her. You go," he said, shoving me towards the door.

I didn't let go of his hand.

"Sidney, I have to get your sister. Please go, I'll be right behind you."

He pulled harder, this time breaking my hold on him, and rushed to the bedroom door.

Once he opened it, I saw him take one giant step forward then stop. Something caught his attention in the room. His back was to me, but I already knew what he saw.

He faced me with confusion in his eyes, and before the smoke completely overtook me I remembered that I told you the first person I killed was Ms. Darcy. Well, I lied. It was Clara.

CHAPTER FOURTEEN

"MY SHOES DIDN'T SURVIVE."

My eyes fluttered open, and it took me a moment to realize I was in a hospital bed.

However, after glancing around the stark white room, hearing doctor pages over the intercom, and the ubiquitous smell of antiseptic attacking my senses, reality set in.

I felt slightly foggy, but okay overall. I turned my head to see a nurse changing out a bag of liquid beside my bed.

"Oh, hi you're awake. How are you feeling?" she asked.

Her voice was light and gentle, and I noticed her name tag had Natalie printed on it.

"I'm okay," I tried to say, but my throat was so dry it hurt.

Natalie noticed my discomfort immediately. She reached for the water on the table beside my bed and poured me a cup, then helped me drink it.

"You breathed in a decent amount of smoke. It's a good thing your boyfriend was there. He got you out even before the firefighters arrived."

It all came flooding back to me. All the smoke, the confusion, Nathan rescuing me and . . . Clara!

Oh, Clara!

"Is he here?" I asked the nurse.

To my relief, she shook her head.

"No. He stepped out to go to the cafeteria. He should be back soon. The doctor will be in as well. Do you need anything for pain?"

I declined the medicine and then asked, "What happened?"

"I'm not completely sure, but from what I understand around 5 pm yesterday a kid that resides in your building somehow started the fire accidentally."

Yesterday?

That meant I'd slept in the hospital for 24 hours after Nathan rescued me.

I vaguely recalled he was supposed to take me to a Japanese restaurant around 5:30 yesterday, which would explain why he was even there in the first place.

But if it weren't for the mischievous brat that set the fire, Gary I assume, none of this would have happened.

"Do you know how bad the damages were?"

Her face looked saddened.

"I'm sorry, they say 95% of the building got destroyed." She rubbed my shoulder, offering comfort. "But the good news is everyone made it out."

Except my fucking shoes! I thought.

I nodded and tried to appear relieved. Even though my shoes didn't survive, at least Mr. Gregory did. That was good news. Although, if I had to choose between the two, it could be a close call.

"You had a few cuts and bruises. We have cleaned them up and I think they should heal quickly. Although the cut on your face may leave some scarring."

My hand instinctively touched my face, and I was reminded of two nights ago with Alexander. I wished I could stab that fucking bastard again.

"Yeah, I think I fell or something trying to get out of the building," I said.

Giving me a sympathetic nod, Natalie adjusted my covers and said, "You need your rest. My name is Natalie and I'll be taking care of you. If you need anything just press the button."

I gave her a weak smile and she left the room. As soon as the door shut behind her, I got out of bed, disconnected my IV and located my bag of belongings.

Damn, no shoes. I guess I'm stuck wearing these thick-padded hospital socks. Oh, well things could be worse.

I rushed to get dressed. I couldn't see Nathan right now or possibly ever again. I knew our time wouldn't last forever, but I didn't think it would be over so soon.

He wouldn't understand. So many people didn't understand.

Barbara understood, as much as I didn't care for her.

Grandma understood because she was a saint, and Lillian understood because... well she's Lillian.

I finished pulling on my pajamas and then realized I also had no phone, no ATM card, no home to return to, and worst of all, no Clara. I hope she's alright.

I found a pair of scissors in one of the drawers and cut off my hospital bracelet. I walked towards the door, noticing a blanket and pillow in the chair. That must have been where Nathan slept, waiting for me to wake up.

I sighed and pushed on. No matter how kind he was, I couldn't stay. I had killed a man, and something tells me this murder won't be as easily written off as the others.

Opening the door, I took a quick peek into the hallway. I didn't see Natalie, but another woman at the nurse's station.

Her back was to me, and now was as good a time as any to get out of here. I walked at a fast pace past the giant white desk and thought that I was completely in the clear when I heard Natalie's voice.

She was exiting a room in front of me, holding a tray and assuring the patient that she would return with their pain medicine.

I stepped into a small opening in the hallway that led to a closet, and Natalie walked right past it without seeing me.

I released a breath I didn't realize I was holding. I hated hospitals, and no good memories ever came from this place.

Too many wasted years during my childhood were spent around people with white coats. I have to get out of here without being seen.

After checking that the coast was clear once again, I darted into the hallway and followed the exit signs out of the building.

Finally, out on the street, I assumed I must've looked like someone that needed to be returned to the hospital. I was wearing blue and gray pajamas, my hair was wild, and my face was bruised.

At the moment I didn't have many options.

Hell, who was I kidding?

I didn't have any options, but I was about to change that. I saw an older woman up ahead sitting at the bus stop.

If anyone was going to feel sorry for me, it's going to be a woman who likely had grandchildren and a soft spot for pitiful-looking people.

"Excuse me," I said.

"Oh dear," she replied, glancing from my messy-looking pajamas to my face. "Are you okay?"

"No. My place burned down and I just got released from the hospital. Do you think you can cover my bus fare so that I can get to the bank on 3rd street?"

She touched her chest.

"You poor girl, of course, I can. The bus should be here

in the next five minutes. I can pay your fare and give you some money to get something to eat."

"Thanks, but I'm not hungry. The bus ride will suffice."

"You have to eat. How else will you regain your strength? You can even come home with me and get cleaned up."

She was definitely a grandmother or wanted to be. Her eagerness to protect and nurture spoke volumes. I smiled at her.

"Thank you, but I have a friend at the bank. She will help me from there."

I had no such friend, but I was familiar with some of the employees there. I had no wallet, which meant no identification or ATM card. Hopefully, they were in a rule-bending mood so that I could get some money and I could get out of town.

"Okay, just promise me you will take care of yourself," she said worriedly.

Lady, protecting myself is a top priority.

"You have my word," I assured her.

Right on schedule, the bus pulled up, and we boarded. I chose a seat towards the back so that I wasn't the center of attention for new passengers, and Mrs. Nell, the kind woman covering my ride today, sat beside me.

I preferred to sit alone, but I understood she wanted to watch over me and possibly have someone to talk to.

Mrs. Nell told me all about her seven kids and fifteen grandchildren, showing me pictures and videos for reference.

They were a beautiful family and appeared to be genuinely happy, something I didn't see a lot.

As the bus took a route I was familiar with, we passed my apartment building, and everything looked so foreign.

The construction, or the shell of what used to be, was something you would expect to see in a disaster movie. Natalie was right; almost the whole building was damaged significantly.

Guess I no longer had to worry about destroying the evidence from my night with Alexander or Marcus, for that matter. If any of it survived, I didn't think it would be too helpful to the police.

The bus had to reroute since the actual road in front of my building was blocked off.

"Oh my," Mrs. Nell gasped from beside me. "It looks worse than I thought. I'm glad you made it out alright."

I could only nod. I was thinking about Clara. I hoped she was okay. I had already lost her once. I didn't want to lose her again.

The bus let me off in front of the bank, and I thanked Mrs. Nell one last time. She gave me her phone number in case I needed any more help, and I was on my way.

I entered the bank, signed in, and took a seat. I received a few awkward stares from other customers that were waiting, but no one said anything.

"Sidney Jacobson?" A man in a dark blue business suit called out.

It was Mr. Nolan, a banker I was familiar with, but more importantly, he was familiar with me. I remember once he said I reminded him of his younger sister in college.

Unless his sister enjoyed killing for sport, he had no idea how far off that comparison was.

I stood and approached him.

"Sidney, are you okay?"

"Yeah," I said, gearing up to tug at someone else's heartstrings for the day. It wasn't hard. Losing everything in a fire was a sad thing, except for me, it was also slightly beneficial.

"What can I do for you?" he asked.

"I need your help. My apartment building burned down and I lost everything. I barely escaped with my life. I need to withdraw some money to go stay with my cousin for a little while."

Mr. Nolan covered his mouth and I watched compassion fill his eyes,

"That's terrible! Step into my office, let's see what we can do."

I followed him inside. He closed the door, and I sat down in front of a large giant oak desk. I rarely came into the private offices.

I usually conducted my business either at the ATM or in the teller line; it was nice in here. Mr. Nolan hit a few keys on his computer before speaking.

"I assume you have no identification, right?"

"Right."

He sighed.

"I'm not supposed to provide access to any accounts without proper ID, but considering the circumstances," he looked me over in my pitiful state. "I think I can bend the rules."

I gave him a grateful smile.

"Please tell me that you at least know your account and social security number?"

I nodded and gave him the requested information. He looked me over again, "I'm sorry you've been through so much, I will also issue you a temporary bank card to help you access your money easier."

"Oh, that won't be necessary," I said.

His brows knitted together.

"Why is that?"

"Because I'd like to withdraw it all."

I had over fifty thousand dollars in my account. I removed all of it except $10,000 and deposited the rest into my grandmother's account. Thankfully, I knew her account number by heart as well.

$10,000 would be enough to get me started in my new life. I planned to find a way to get to the other side of the country and then out of it completely.

I would need an ID to purchase the plane ticket, which I didn't have, but I was sure I could find someone to create a fake one for me somewhere.

Mr. Nolan was kind enough to drop me off at a trucker stop right off the highway that was attached to a souvenir shop.

He also gave me a rather stylish-looking black pouch that I could carry my cash in because he felt nervous with me walking around with that much money.

I didn't share in his unease; I welcomed draining the life out of anyone else that got in my way.

At the souvenir shop, I picked up some clothes, shoes, two prepaid phones, and a pack of razor blades. I would resize the blades and put the protective covering over them later.

For now, simply having them in my back pocket made a world of difference.

Checking my reflection in a mirror located in the snack section, I frowned. I looked like I didn't possess one ounce of fashion sense.

I was wearing an ugly black hoodie with a bear on it, pink stretch pants with purple hearts, and beige slide-on shoes that reminded me of a nurse from the '70s.

My frown deepened as I continued to stare.

I don't need to go to jail. Being forced to wear these shoes is punishment enough for my crimes.

Pulling myself away from the train wreck, which was my current outfit, I went outside and sat on a bench. There was a bus station downtown, I would make my way there to start my journey.

A couple walked into the gas station holding hands, and I was reminded of the next thing I needed to do. I pulled out one of the prepaid phones and dialed Nathan's number.

He answers on the second ring.

"Hi, Nathan."

"Sidney!! Thank God. I've been worried about you. I came back to the hospital room and you were gone. Where are you?"

"I'm safe."

"Safe? Sidney, where are you? I will come and get you right now."

"I only called to say goodbye."

"Goodbye? Sidney . . . " he stopped. He was searching for the words, I could tell. "What are you talking about?"

"You're a good guy. Always stay that way."

"Come on, you have to help me out here. What's going on? Why are you saying goodbye?"

"It's complicated."

I prepared to hang up when I heard him ask, "Is this about Clara?"

I said nothing, and Nathan must have taken that as his opening to ask more questions. He was obviously filled with them and had been doing a lot of thinking.

"Why was the bedroom empty in your apartment Sidney? There was no furniture, no clothes, nothing. I thought your sister lived with you. Did she move out? Or . . ."

He stopped again, not wanting to say his next words.

"She isn't real, is she? It would explain so much. All of your secrecy. Why I've never seen her or even spoken to her."

My continued silence solidified his fear.

"Aww baby, we can get you some help. I love you, you just have to trust me. Tell me where you are."

I closed my eyes. His voice and words were so raw, genuine, and well-intentioned, but he didn't understand.

I knew he wouldn't understand. He sounded like all those doctors from my childhood, telling me she didn't exist and trying to force their beliefs on me.

"723 Langston Drive. Repeat it back to me," I said.

He did and then followed up with, "Okay I'm on my way."

I could hear keys rattling.

"I'm not there."

"What? I don't understand."

"That's my grandmother's address. I need you to go there and check on her. She may be able to answer questions you have."

"Sidney! Wait—"

"Tell her that I will contact her as soon as I can and that the money I deposited into her account should be enough to take care of her for a while."

"Please, don't do this," I heard his voice breaking, but I couldn't help him. I couldn't comfort him.

He was on his own as much as it seemed that I was on mine.

CHAPTER FIFTEEN

"TIME OF DEATH, 3:45PM

We were three years old when it happened. The memory itself was hazy, as if it was a secret box that belonged to someone else, and I was able to peek inside and steal glances.

Clara and I were with Lillian at some guy's house. I didn't know exactly why we were there, although now I could probably make a guess.

However, I do remember that we weren't allowed inside under any circumstances.

He had a pool in the backyard and a small play area. We would be left there with a bag of snacks and a few toys until Lillian came to get us hours later.

On one particular day, I returned from peeing behind a tall bush and spotted Clara playing with my favorite barbie doll.

Even now, I could feel the rage that engulfed me at watching her touch my things. The anger seemed more alive than the memory itself. I guess I always had a temper problem.

Either way, I chased her near the pool and struggled to pull it out of her grasp. Eventually, I shoved her hard and broke her hold on it, and went about my merry way. I had my toy, and that was all that mattered.

This was where that part of the memory goes blank.

Sometime later, I asked Lillian when Clara would come back because I missed her.

Lillian slapped me and said that Clara was never coming back because I killed her. I didn't understand, but I never asked about Clara again.

I went on with my life, accepting the loneliness, the fear, and the torture being dealt out by a mother who didn't love me and an uncle who was every kid's nightmare.

I bottled up the pain and the rage, tucking it deep down inside because I was too small to do much else.

I went to see doctors who asked me questions about Clara, why I hurt her, and things about my life at home, but I mostly stayed quiet and colored or played with the colorful blocks they gave me.

Lillian didn't need to warn me again about keeping my mouth shut.

Then one day, when I was seven, after a horrible visit from my uncle and his roaming hands. I found a bottle of Lillian's pills that she left in the bathroom.

The word written on the bottle was long and complicated, and I had no idea what it was prescribed for, but I figured it should do the trick.

I heard Lillian on the phone once, and she said that her friend died from an overdose of pills. I wasn't sure if these were those pills, but I hoped so.

I checked the clock and said to myself, "Time of death, 3:45 pm".

It was an odd thing for a seven-year-old to say, but it was what the doctors always announced on those medical shows when they pronounced someone dead.

I held the bottle up to the light. It was half full. Opening the top, I poured a pill out into my hand. It was really tiny.

If I wanted it to work, I figured I'd better take them all. I lifted my hand to my mouth and just before I took it I heard someone call my name.

"Sidney!"

In my startled state, I dropped the pills, and they rolled everywhere. I spun around, thinking I would see Lillian, but instead, I saw Clara.

"What are you doing?" she asked me.

"I . . . I was coming to be with you?"

"Why would you do that when I'm already here?"

"But . . . they . . . they said that I killed you."

"They don't know what they are talking about. You only killed my body, I can exist without that."

I stared at her, my sister, my twin, who I hadn't seen in years, but like me, she had aged.

"How are you here? This must not be real."

"I'm real. I've been watching you all these years. I know how they have hurt you, and when you were alone, I would sit with you, but it wasn't until now that I was strong enough for you to see me."

Tears fell down my face. I rushed to hug her but felt nothing more than air.

"Why can't I touch you?"

Clara shrugged.

"I think that's just the way it works. My body is gone."

I looked down at the floor. The despair and ache in my heart were more painful than ever before.

"That means you can't stay," I mumbled.

"Yes, I can. We can share your body and I'll be with you forever."

And ever since, she has been. I smile at the fond memory. Initially, we only talked.

Clara was there every day when I was alone, getting me

through the rough patches and helping me to survive Lillian and the insane world that held me hostage.

But when I was ten, something wonderful happened. Lillian was arrested for murder and signed over parental rights to grandma Nancy. At that time, Clara's return was still a secret to everyone except me.

That all changed when I went to a youth summer camp. Grandma thought the experience would do me some good, and Clara thought it would be a great time to explore the world on her own, but things didn't go so well.

That bitch Selena teased her and hurt Clara's feelings, and I snapped. People had been dishing out hurt all my life. It was finally time to see if any of them could take it.

Unfortunately, Selena survived, and when I told the camp counselors why I did it, I was referred to doctors that labeled me a psycho. Alright, I'm not being fair.

Technically I was diagnosed with a dissociative identity disorder, but see!

That's the same thing, right?

According to them, the trauma from my childhood triggered me to create another identity. I recall one of the sessions I had with Dr. Gordon at the age of sixteen.

I awoke to him watching me, similar to the way Barbara was watching me that day. I was lying on a soft blue couch inside his office. If I miss anything about my hospital days it was that couch.

"What is your name?" he had asked me.

I squinted at him.

"You know my name."

"Humor me."

I rolled my eyes. We went through this several times a week.

"Sidney Jacobson," I said, letting the annoyance his question stirred in me accompany my reply.

He checked his watch.

"Less than five minutes ago. You said your name was Clara. It is what you have been saying all morning. Yet, for some reason, at 3:45, you say your name is Sidney."

I eyed his metal envelope opener. It was brass-colored, long, and sharp; I'd like to bury it in his eye.

"What's your point, doc?"

He remained calm like he always did upon my snappy reply.

“Your IQ is off the charts, and your particular case of dissociative disorder is quite remarkable and evolved. The differences between you and the other identity are equipped with such distinguishing behavior, memory, and thinking it's nothing short of extraordinary."

"Layman's terms for the disinterested, please," I said with a sigh.

His session always lasted way too long.

"For one," he said, giving me a somewhat interesting look, "the other identity is a lot more tolerable. And according to our examinations, even though you can't recall details when the other identity has taken over, you are very much aware of it, and you've created a fascinating bond."

"What can I say? I'm easy to get along with."

Dr. Gordon placed his judgmental chart of notes on the small table beside him, crossed his legs and removed his glasses.

"This is not to be taken lightly, Sidney. With your family history of mental issues and abuse, over time, you could start having blackouts and become more assertive and possibly violent until eventually the more dominant identity takes control and pushes the other away completely."

I balled up my fist and wondered who would miss Dr. Gordon if I ended his life now. He had no idea about my desire to kill, and at the time, I hadn't intentionally taken a life.

It had been years since the occurrence at camp with Selena, and the entire medical team was convinced that the situation was an isolated incident that proper treatment could resolve. They were wrong.

"You seem upset, Sidney. Why?"

"Oh, I don't know, maybe because you're implying that Clara will leave."

"But Clara isn't real, Sidney. We have been over this. She died when you were three."

I didn't know why they kept reminding me of that. I understood what happened to Clara, I had accepted the terrible thing I'd done. But someway, somehow, my sister was with me now, and no one would ever change that.

I looked him straight in the eyes and said, "Well, I guess she didn't get the memo."

A car honked its horn at someone crossing the street on their way into the souvenir shop, and it yanked me from the memory of my time with Dr. Gordon.

I suddenly realized I was gripping the arm of the bench too tight and let go. I usually suppressed the memories of my stay at the clinic.

Those asshats were so fucking aggravating. But I did learn to be careful, say what they needed to hear, and behave as expected. Besides, the Selena's of the world couldn't squeal on me if they were dead.

Several years later, I was able to stop seeing a counselor on a regular basis, and they lowered the dosage of my meds.

Unbeknownst to them, I decided to lower them completely by flushing them down the toilet. I would protect Clara and me no matter what, and no one would ever cross me again.

When grandma learned that Clara was still with me at

18, she found herself at a crossroads. All she wanted was for the suffering I had endured to stop.

Therefore, she could either try to obtain rights to get me admitted or let me live my life.

Ultimately she chose the latter, convincing herself that I'd already been through enough and I wasn't harming anyone, her words not mine. I was hurting plenty of people, and I liked it.

Nonetheless, both Clara and I promised that we would check in regularly and stay out of trouble.

Grandma had her doubts, I was sure, but in the end, believing that I was better was easier.

My grandma also provided updates to Lillian about my condition and progress over the years.

However, Lillian was not at all surprised when Clara came to visit her. She knew their methods wouldn't work.

Hell, if they couldn't fix her, she didn't believe for a second that they could fix me.

The visits with Lillian and Clara didn't last long, though. Lillian was a monster and intimidated Clara; therefore I had to take over.

Moving forward, Clara was happy, and so was I. She enrolled in college to become a pediatrician and mostly stayed to herself until she eventually found a friend in Barbara and confided in her.

Barbara was familiar with our supposed disorder and wanted to help. She had what I called practice sessions with Clara but never a sit down with me. I didn't have time for that shit. I was done being examined.

I told Clara it wasn't smart to trust Barbara, but I couldn't control her life. She uses our body during the day, and I usually take over as it gets closer to night. 3:45 to 4 pm seemed to be our sweet spot for changing shifts.

Thankfully, Barbara turned out to be harmless. She

knew Clara for years and never said anything about our secret. I think she was intrigued by how different Clara and I were both in appearance and personality.

For example, when Clara used our body, she had her own identity.

She wore a wig with a different hair color than mine, contacts, and I taught her how to do makeup with slight contouring so that she could highlight her own natural features.

Then, because she preferred the more sophisticated look, Clara wore non-prescription glasses and dressed a lot more conservatively than yours truly.

Also, thanks to Clara's smart thinking and some people willing to ask no questions for the right price, we got Clara her own ID and added her to the lease.

We did a phenomenal job of representing ourselves, and it showed, Barbara had no idea in the beginning. Over time, I think the differences stood out much easier.

One thing I always wondered though, through all of her analyzing techniques, did Barbara suspect I was a murderer? I never asked, and I know Clara never told.

That was our little secret, one that we would take to our graves. I was so blessed to have a sister like Clara.

I didn't know what I would do without her, except now I feared, as I sat on this bench alone trying to plan out my next move, I might have to find out.

"No you won't. I'm not going anywhere."

My head snapped to the right.

"Clara! Where in the hell have you been?"

"Overwhelmed! The fire, knowing Alexander kidnapped you and wondering how we will escape getting caught? Sleep was my only outlet."

I narrowed my eyes at her.

"Okay, please end the suspense. How do you always know what I've been up to when I haven't told you?"

Clara smiled at me.

"Alright, I'll tell you. It's because you dream about it. When you're sleeping and I'm using the body, I catch glimpses of your dreams."

"Wow, that's cool. Why can't I do that with you?"

"It's my gift I guess and a good thing too because you can't be trusted to stay out of trouble."

"That's fair. You're about to lecture me aren't you?"

"On the contrary little sister, I want to thank you. You do a great job protecting us."

I laughed at her use of little sister.

"I'm only a minute younger and you're welcome. I guess my moving idea doesn't sound so bad now does it?"

Clara sighed.

"No, I think it's our best plan. I'm just worried about grandma."

"I know what you mean. I'm sure she's going to be okay Clara."

Clara shook her head and stared out at the clear blue sky.

She was silent for a long time before saying, "I think I'm going to leave the living to you for a while. But I'll be here if you need me. And Sidney," she said, pointing a finger at me. "Try to stay out of trouble. No murder unless it's mandatory."

"But it's so fun Clara."

"What am I going to do with you?"

"I don't know, love me the way I am?" I offered with a grin.

"Always sister," she smiled. "Listen, I'm about to zone out. Do we have enough money for where we're going?"

Yup."

"And you have a plan?"

"Got us covered."

"What about your blades?"

"In my back pocket."

"Alright, looks like we're good to go . . . except . . ."

She looked down, a sad expression covered her face.

"What's wrong?" I asked.

"I wanted to say goodbye to Barbara. Not now of course, but eventually I wanted to call her and say thank you. She's been a really good friend."

"Good thing I got an extra prepaid phone for you to call her once we are settled far, far away."

The happiness in her eyes made my day a million times better.

"Thanks, Sidney. You're the best."

"I know."

I stood up.

"I guess we better get out of here. There's a bus stop down the street."

Clara was nodding her agreement when a huge truck stopped in front of us.

The driver leaned over and peered down out the passenger window.

He was old, fat, and sweaty looking.

He probably thought he could get some action. I'll bet all his money went to prostitutes.

"Hey, are you looking for a ride?"

"No, I'm good."

I began to walk away. He chuckled.. It sounded grimy and dismissive.

"Come on sweet cheeks, I won't bite."

I stopped. Pet names from sleazy guys pissed me the fuck off. I turned to the trucker and smiled.

"Don't hurt him," Clara whispered to me.

"Relax Clara. What's one more for the road?"

About the Author

Nicki Grace is an Atlanta native with a bachelor's in business and a Masters in Marketing. As a wife, mother, author and designer, she is addicted to writing, spas, laughing, and sex jokes, but not exactly in that order.

Her comedic personality and unique upbringing by an illiterate but fiercely strong mother and a courageous, prideful father, made her view of the world pretty unconventional.

Luckily for you, someone gave her internet access, and now you get to experience all the EMOTIONAL, EXCITING, SHOCKING, and HOT ideas that reside in her head. She loves to have fun and lives for a good story. And we're guessing so do you! Nickigracenovels.com

facebook.com/nickigracenovels
instagram.com/nickigracenovels
tiktok.com/@nickigracenovels
BB bookbub.com/authors/nicki-grace

USE THE QR CODE BELOW TO VISIT MY WEBSITE

Romance

The Inevitable Encounters Series

Book 1: The Hero of my Love Scene

Book 2: The Love of my Past, Present

Book 3 : The Right to my Wrong

The Love Is Series

Book 1: Love is Sweet

Book 2: Love is Sour

Book 3: Love is Salty

Erotica

His Mouthpiece

His Mouthpiece: The Prequel

This Side of Wrong

Thrillers

Break Him

The Twisted Damsel

The Darkest Damsel

Women's Fiction

Cut off Your Nose to Spite Your Face

The Splintered Doll (A Memoir)

Self-Help

The TIPSY COUNSELOR Series

The Tipsy Dating Counselor (Summary)

Book 1: The Tipsy Dating Counselor (UNRATED)

Book 2: The Tipsy Marriage Counselor

Book 3: The Pregnancy Counselor

Printed in Great Britain
by Amazon